WORLDS COLLIDE

WORLDS AWAY: BOOK TWO

JL HENDRICKS

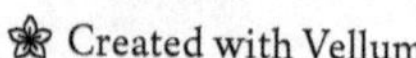

OTHER BOOKS BY J.L. HENDRICKS

<u>New Orleans Magic</u>

Book 0: Magic's Not Real

Book 1: New Orleans Magic

Book 2: Hurricane of Magic

Book 3: Council of Magic

<u>Alpha Alien Abduction Tales Series</u>

Book 0: Worlds Revealed (join my Newsletter to get this exclusive freebie)

Book 1: Worlds Away

Book 2: Worlds Collide

Book 2.5: Worlds Explode

Book 3: Worlds Entwined

<u>A Shifter Christmas Romance Series (Miss Claus)</u>

Book 0: Santa Meets Mrs. Claus

Book 1: Miss Claus and the Secret Santa

Book 2: Miss Claus under the Mistletoe

Book 3: Miss Claus and the Christmas Wedding

Book 4: Miss Claus and Her Polar Opposite

<u>The FBI Dragon Chronicles</u>

Book 1: A Ritual of Fire

Book 2: A Ritual of Death

Book 3: A Ritual of Conquest

<u>Chronicles of the Unwanted Princess</u>

Book 1: The Portal of Chance

Book 2: The Forbidden Portal

Book 3: The Emerald Portal

<u>Mr. Claus series coming Christmas 2021</u>

See these titles and more at https://www.jlhendricksauthor.com/

This book is part of a series and best read in the following order, although each book is complete with an HEA and no cliffhangers:

Worlds Away Series
    Book 1 – Worlds Away
    Book 2 – Worlds Collide
    Worlds Revealed – Book 0.5 (join my newsletter to get this book free)
    Book 2.5 – Worlds Explode (could be read in any order after book 2)
    Book 3 – Worlds Entwined

CHAPTER ONE

"Natalie, you are with me today. We need to scour the back section of the ship for supplies while we wait for the Star Prime to arrive." Zelan pointed to me as I sat in the cramped corner of the room I had been staying in since the Zamaya crashed on this alien planet after the space battle.

Those of us who were too stupid to get away once the ship crashed had all been corralled and brought to the front of the ship. We were all split up into different rooms and sections. Some even had to sleep in the corridor. I didn't know many of the women in this section because most of them had been in the other room of abductees. The aliens called that room Beta, and ours was called Alpha. They were so original with their names. However, I was making friends.

I missed Paris and Sheila, two of the women I met after being abducted by the huge, alpha aliens. They had become my friends. Zelan told me Paris was really busy with her assignment as a medic. I didn't know she had a medical background. I had thought she was homeless. Maybe living on the streets gave her a quick medical background?

"Where are we going today? And please tell me you guys

have killed all of those giant insects. I don't think I can take another one touching me, even if you do kill it. That stuff they discharge when you kill them takes forever to come out and stinks something awful!"

Yesterday, when we were out scavenging the ship, we came across three insectoids inside our ship who were ravaging our supplies. They were stuffing their backpack shaped bags with medical supplies as well as with our food bars. I thought that their ship must have taken a lot of damage for them to come over here during the day. Zelan thought they had been here all night and were waiting for the sun to set before setting off back to their ship.

The mutant insectoids, the Zateelians, who invaded our ship after shooting it down from space, didn't like the sunlight. They could stand to be outside for a little while, but not too long. It is thought that the sun hurts their eyes. The rest of their body seems to be very strong. I know this because it took three shots from Zelan to kill one of them who had me pinned down on the ground. It slathered some goo on me, into my face to be precise, and then was backing away. My guess is it knew that the next shot was going to kill it, and it did. This then put more of that slime on my body. I couldn't win, even when they died. After that, we went straight to the med-bay where the doctor examined me and proclaimed me clean.

What was that all about?

I was covered in that disgusting, viscous discharge the bug left all over the top half of my body. I was NOT clean. However, everyone around me seemed to breathe out at once, like they had all been holding their breath. I needed a twenty-minute shower to get all of that slime off but was only given ten minutes. I swear my hair still smelled of mutant cockroach slime.

Today should have been about me resting and recovering, I still had a bump on my head from when that creature attacked me and caused me to fall back to the hard ground. I couldn't sleep all night thinking about the creature that almost ate me. Now Zelan wants me to go back out with him again?

Is he crazy?

CHAPTER TWO

"Great! Out of one jail cell and into another. Natalie, I thought that we were done with that? Why can't the Commander let us stay in rooms instead of forcing us in here?" Betsy asked me as we were herded like cattle into our new "accommodations," as the new captain called them.

Accommodations? Yeah right!

The *Star Prime* arrived today. We had been sent over to the other ship. While it was damaged in the space battle with the Zateelians, it made its way to the planet mostly unscathed. It was in much better shape than our ship. So, it was decided that we all needed to head over there.

Betsy had wrapped her arms around her middle section, and I could see she was holding back tears. We had spent the past couple of days on Commander Venay's ship and helped them to round up supplies and even take care of the wounded. Paris was really in her element acting as a medic on the bridge with the Commander watching her every move. We deserved better treatment than this.

"Betsy, I don't know. Maybe we can ask Paris when we see her next. If things go back to the way they were, then I bet she'll bring us our meals again." I tried to offer her a smile, but I didn't think it came out very well.

"Natalie, these cells are even smaller than the other ones. How are we going to spend 5 months cooped up here while we wait for our abductors to bring in a new ship?" Betsy had been complaining non-stop since we made our way to the new ship.

But I couldn't fault her for it, I wasn't much better.

The ship we were on originally had been broken up into three pieces after we crash landed on this alien world. It was fit to live in, plus the Zateelians were constantly coming over and attacking us. No one told me, but I think we lost a couple warriors and some more humans to the mutant cockroaches. They were scary and intimidating.

I shivered whenever I thought about their cockroach/grasshopper hybrid bodies. They could walk on their back appendages as well as on all fours. We had to constantly scan the ground as well as the ceilings since they could also scale the walls and walk above us.

Zelan caught one on the ceiling the other day and he killed it before it crawled close enough to attack us.

"I wish I knew." I huffed out and looked up to the ceiling. My right hand automatically made its way to my forehead while my left one tried to rest on my hip. At least there wasn't a chance the insectoids were crawling around above us here.

We were so tightly squished in here that my elbow hit someone else on their back, "Sorry about that." I dropped my arms to my sides in silent misery.

The new male warriors served our evening meal. I didn't recognize any of them from my time on Commander Venay's ship. They must be from our new prison ship, the *Star Prime*. It was that stupid, chalky, jello garbage that we had when we were first abducted. "Hey, why are you feeding us this garbage? Where's Paris? She used to bring us Earth food." I asked one of the new warriors on guard duty.

"This is standard fare for slaves. Be happy that you are getting anything at all," he stated with zero emotion in his voice. He sounded more like an android than a person. But then again, this was a regular soldier who was accustomed to fighting and picking out slaves. Not one of the slave trade warriors who made regular trips to Earth and was comfortable with us.

Over the past week, we had started to make quasi-friendships with a few of the warriors who guarded us on a regular basis. Somehow, I doubted these new guys would become our friends.

"Can I ask where Paris is?" If I could talk with her, maybe we could get better food and accommodations.

"She is spending time with the Commander. They are to be mated tomorrow," Mr. Personality said.

"Really? Already? Isn't it a bit soon?" My jaw dropped as my hands flew in the air and bounced down on my thighs, hitting someone in the process. I mumbled an apology, but she didn't even register I'd hit her.

"No, it is not. If this is what they want, then now is the perfect time. Our Captain can take good care of this ship without the Commander." He sounded like he wasn't too happy with the Commander taking over.

"Oh, I see how it is. You don't like the Commander, do you?" I eyed him up and down as he squirmed before answering me.

"There is nothing wrong with the Commander. I just do not know him. But it is safer for his mate to go through with the ceremony. Once that happens, no one on this ship will touch her. She will be treated like a queen. You might want to consider your options as well. Spending the next five months in these packed cells will not be pleasant." He spun on his heels, walked over to the next cell, and ignored my requests to get a message to Paris.

"Hmph, maybe Sheila or Lisa will come visit us tomorrow, Betsy." I narrowed my eyes at that guard and decided that he was definitely not going to be the warrior I would mate with, if I ever did.

The next morning Zelan was part of the group who brought us our breakfast. I never thought I would be happy to see him, but I was. "Zelan, is there any way to get better food on this ship? Seriously, even the ration bars would be better than this stuff." I scooped some up with my spoon and let it drop back onto my plate in white, sticky, globs. I didn't know how much longer my stomach would allow this as sustenance before it revolted.

"Natalie, their food replicators do not have recipes for Earth food. This is all the lead warrior will allow us to bring you." He dropped his head and then looked back up at me. "Unless, would you agree to be my mate? I could protect you better that way, and you could find more palatable food."

"Um, thank you, but...I," I tried to shuffle my feet, but there was very little room while most of the women in my cell sat down. "I'm still hoping to go home to my fiancé. I thought that we might somehow make it off this planet and back to Earth." I couldn't look him in the eye. I knew he had an attraction for me; he must have since he chose me every day to go out with him and scavenge the old ship.

"I am sorry, but you will never make it back to Earth. I hope you realize that soon and start thinking about a future with me." He moved off to the next cell of women and gave them their breakfast. All I could hear was soft "ugh's" and "not again" as the warriors fed the rest of my prison mates. Normally they chatted with us. I had guessed that things on this ship were going to be a whole lot different than before. And sadly, I was right.

There was no way I was going to become a mate to some alien who had abducted me from my perfect life back home. Well, okay it wasn't perfect. But it was my life! One I wanted so desperately to have back.

CHAPTER THREE

After a couple of days, Paris came to see us. She was with the group of warriors who brought us food, but today was different. Most of the warriors were ones I recognized, including Zelan.

"Paris!" I yelled as soon as I saw her. She came over to my cell with a great big smile on her face. "Does that smile mean we are going home soon?" I asked hopefully.

"No, I'm sorry. I wish I had better news for you. I'm just happy to see you and to know you're okay." She reached into my cell and tried to hug me, but with the women and bars so close, it was an awkward attempt.

"I heard you got married. Was that what you wanted? It happened awfully fast." I scrunched up my nose and wondered how horrible her honeymoon must have been. That big, huge giant of a man. It had to be terrible.

She blushed a bit and smiled as she looked down at the ground. "It was actually quite wonderful. I couldn't have asked for a better mate. He is so gentle and loving when it is just the two of us. Venay is a completely different man when we are alone. I think I'm falling in love with him." Her smile broadened even more as she looked up at me with a sparkle in her eyes.

"Oh great, another one who drank the Kool-Aid. While you were gone, three more of the girls agreed to mate with the aliens. I think the guys were all from the Commander's original ship too. I guess it makes sense with us all being so close this past week, but now that we're in prison again, I'm more inclined to tell the next guy to piss off rather than agree to a mating. Why can't we be let free here? Most of us were very helpful before the new ship came and took us." I felt claustrophobic in this tight cell. I couldn't even move around to express my feelings because we were packed tighter than sardines.

"Natalie, you should really reconsider. Venay's guys, for the most part, are really great. I have worked very closely with them since the crash and made some friends. You might want to consider marrying one of them, and soon. Life is going to be very tough if you stay in this cage for the next five months." She gave me a quick smile while she squeezed my hand. "I gotta get everyone else fed. Sorry, I couldn't bring you guys anything better, but I'm working with Venay to get some of the replicators from his old ship brought over here so we can have better food."

With that, she walked away from me. I didn't see her again until later in the day. It was so boring now. All I could do was twiddle my thumbs to waste away the time, and even that was tough to do while being so tightly packed.

After lunch, Zelan came to visit me. I was actually happy to see him, which was weird because I had no desire to mate with him. However, I did seem to miss him when he wasn't around. Maybe it was because we spent so much time this past week doing stuff together, instead of sitting in a crowded cell. Either way, I couldn't keep the smile off my face as he walked toward me.

His eyes sparkled, and his smile was so big, it made me

feel all soft inside. Something about him made my heart skip a beat. He was a good looking male. If I had to guess, I would say he was at least six feet, eight inches tall. It was hard to calculate since I wasn't used to seeing men that tall back on Earth.

My fiancé, Ben, was about my height. Without heels, I equaled his five feet, six inches. Whenever I went out with him, I wasn't allowed to wear heels. He hated it if I was taller than him, even if it was only because of my heels. My girl-friends used to say he had *short man's syndrome*, whatever that meant.

As each day passed, I started to miss Ben less and less, but I continued to miss my family. Would I ever get home? Doubtful. But I had no idea what to do about it, yet.

"Natalie, I have a proposition for you." Zelan walked up to where I was and grabbed ahold of the bars. The fingers on his left hand brushed up against my cheek. His veins were pulsing purple. I had noticed that they pulsed various colors, even spoke about it with the other girls in our group, but no one knew what the colors meant.

"Hi, Zelan, what do you have in mind?" I hoped it wasn't a marriage, or mating, proposal again. While I was happy to see him, it didn't mean that I wanted to marry him.

"I received permission to take you and a couple of the other women with me today on a scouting mission. We are going to go to the old ship and pull out a couple of the food replicators so that you can have better meals. On the way there, we are going to check out what might be a hiding place that houses a few more humans. There are still almost thirty unaccounted for, and it is too dangerous to let them stay out there all alone. Besides the insectoids, this place is home to a few animals that would attack any of us if given the chance."

"Oh, then why are you bringing us? Isn't it dangerous to go out there now?" I couldn't believe he wanted me to go out into that crazy jungle. And with some insectoids still out there too.

"I will be able to protect you. We are bringing two squads of warriors with us. I thought you might enjoy getting out of this place, and helping me to find, and save, some of your friends." His smile was waning, and the color of his veins started to pulse blue. The beautiful purple was gone.

I wanted the purple to come back. Some instinct took over, and I reached my hand out to him. As soon as I realized what I was doing, I pulled back. "Okay, sure. As long as you don't let any of those bugs near me again. Seriously, I still have that smell on me and can't seem to get it off. I don't want to add any more of that slime to my body."

He chuckled, and I was filled with joy. Which was odd, since this was not the place to feel joy. However, it was the first time I had heard anything like a laugh from him, and I liked it.

He let me and a few other women out of the cells. Two of them I had met- Lucy and Betty, and the third I did not know. I walked up to her and introduced myself, "Hi, I'm Natalie." I stuck my hand out and she gave me a good, hearty shake. She had some strength in her grip.

"My name is Rachelle. Nice to meet you." The second she let go of my hand, her head turned toward Zelan. "Oh Zelan, I'm so glad you insisted I accompany you on this mission. I'm ready to help you any way I can." She eyed him up and down and drew nearer to his body. She was practically in his arms.

He smiled down at her, looked up at me, and the smile was wiped off his face. Zelan took two steps back from her, turned around, and started walking out of the holding cell area.

Rachelle looked back at me and smirked, then ran to catch up to him.

"Lucy, what was that all about? Is Rachelle trying to get

Zelan to choose her?" I asked. Then I looked over to Lucy as she laughed and shook her head.

"Oh Natalie, don't you see it? You're her competition. Be careful with that one. She can come off really nice and sweet, until you cross her. If she wants Zelan, she'll do whatever she has to. I was in her cage when we were first abducted. In the beginning, she was like all of us, ticked off that we had been abducted by aliens." She looked over to Rachelle and Zelan who weren't too far away, then lowered her voice a bit more.

"But as soon as she saw how well Paris and the others were treated, she began looking for a mate. She wanted Cazon, but he was too into Sheila to pay attention to any of us. So, she turned her sights to Zelan. He was assigned to our holding area a lot, so she flirted with him every chance she got. And he flirted with her real good too. I thought for sure he would choose her. After the crash, things changed, and he hardly paid Rachelle any attention." Lucy winked.

"Huh, I wonder what happened?" I mused as we followed behind at a discreet distance from Rachelle and Zelan.

"You don't know? It's quite obvious to everyone else. Zelan wants you. Look at his veins. They are flashing an orange color. He never flashes that color with you, does he?" She nodded toward Zelan as we continued to follow him and the new girl.

"No, he's usually purple. Earlier he was blue, and that made me sad. I was happy when he laughed and turned purple again... Have you figured out the colors yet?" I hadn't figured it out yet, but I was beginning to think purple meant he was happy, and blue meant sad, but the other colors still confused me.

"Not yet, but I have an idea. Betty and I have been paying attention to the aliens and their colors. We think they are tied to their emotions. Zelan used to flush a bit of green, and sometimes even purple, when flirting with Rachelle, but lately it has been more orange." Lucy's confirmation on the colors being tied to their emotions really had my interest peeked.

Betty jumped in at this point, she had come up to my other side and whispered her thoughts, "I think orange is frustration or maybe anger. Although, I did see one warrior flush black once, and that was when a guy grabbed Paris and hurt her arm. However, I was across the room, so can't be sure it really was black."

That reminded me of the insects I fought a few days ago. "Wait, I saw Zelan flash black once. We were scavenging on the old ship, and a couple of cockroaches attacked me. His veins turned black as he viciously killed them. I was happy he did because one had crawled up my body and spit out some sort of goo onto my face. It was the most disgusting thing I have ever experienced in my life! I still have nightmares about it." I shivered just thinking about that day.

"Oh, so that's what has you tossing and turning at night. I wondered if it was just our situation. I can understand after being attacked by giant, mutant, cockroach-grasshopper bugs, you wouldn't sleep well. That would be enough to put me in a catatonic state for quite some time!" Lucy wiggled her arms and stuck her tongue out while she hunched her shoulders. She was totally grossed out, but who wouldn't be when faced with what I went through?

"I only saw one from a distance when the warriors picked me up from the old prison cells. We were making our way out, and there were three of them trying to climb up to us, but the warriors shot them. It took several tries too. Their exoskeletons are really tough! It was rather surprising that only the head shots killed them," Betty recollected. She rubbed her hands on her arms and scrunched up her nose.

Zelan turned around at that moment and noticed all of us a bit freaked out from sharing our encounters with the Zateelians. "What's wrong? Why the weird faces?" He cocked his head to one side while looking at each of us.

"Oh, it's nothing. We were just sharing our stories of the past week and those disgusting bugs. I honestly don't know how you guys can fight them and not be freaked out by what they are." I shivered again just thinking about the one who had its head blown off when it was over my stomach.

Zelan chuckled and walked towards me, "Natalie, I promised you I would keep you safe, and I meant it. You don't need to worry. In fact, I would be happy to stay next to you this entire trek. Would that make you feel better?" He put his hand on my shoulder, and I started to calm down. His veins went from pulsing orange to a beautiful shade of green, and he matched the trees around us.

We made our way outside and stopped while we waited for the two squads of warriors to take their place around us. There must have been twenty warriors. Three took point, three took rear, and the rest were spread out along the edge of our small group. I did feel better.

I noticed a couple of friendly faces in our protectors as well. "Hi, Cazon! How's Sheila? And why isn't she with us on this expedition?"

"Hi, Natalie. She is helping Paris with something. I think they are trying to figure out some better meals for you guys until we can get the new food replicators online. Sheila had me try that stuff we normally feed humans, and I can understand why you wouldn't want to eat it." He chuckled as he moved forward in the group.

"Yes, that chalky jello stuff is *not* what I want to eat for dinner tonight. The food ration bars are much better, but that isn't saying much." My stomach turned sour just thinking about the stuff they called *food*.

Zelan looked at me and his veins pulsed purple for a few minutes. That is, until Rachelle interrupted us.

I needed to find a way to keep him purple. There was something calming and assuring about that color on him. The way I felt when he flushed purple, and even green was something I liked. It was almost like drinking chamomile tea on a cool fall evening, relaxing.

"Zelan, I thought you were going to stay by my side for this journey?" She pouted her lips and coyly looked up at him through her eyelashes. I wondered if he knew what she was doing. Her attempts to attract him didn't seem to be working.

He yelled out, "Telan, come here." A very imposing warrior, he must have been as tall as the Commander. He had to be close to seven feet; however, his shoulders weren't as wide. Still, this warrior was strong and very good looking. "I want you to meet Rachelle. She would feel safer if a warrior kept an eye on her today. Would you mind staying close to her?"

"Rachelle, this is Telan. He is one of my best warriors. He will be sure to take good care of you today." Zelan introduced them, but Rachelle didn't seem happy. She gave me a fake smile, tilted her head, and gave a very insincere little laugh.

She did, however, look Telan up and down very slowly. When she reached his chest, I noticed a small smile forming on her lips, and she reached out her hand to touch him. "Well, Telan, you certainly are a strong specimen, aren't you?"

"I would prefer it if you didn't touch me. Your protection is my responsibility, and touching me will not help you," Telan gruffed out. Then he put his hand on her lower back and pushed her forward. The rest of us moved along as well.

I noticed we were headed in a different direction from the old ship. We seemed to be making our own trail now. The way to the old ship had a well, worn path. Probably from so many trips back and forth already. Zelan had told me that they were trying to get everything they could out of the old ship and over to the new one before the insectoids cleaned it out.

They weren't sure, but the latest estimate was that there were most likely still over 150 Zateelians on this planet, all close by. Weren't we the lucky ones! Humph. Yeah right. The sooner we got this mission over with, the better. While I appreciated being out of the super cramped cell, I did not want to encounter another mutant cockroach for as long as I lived!

CHAPTER FOUR

The planet was warm, if I had to guess, maybe mid-eighties. The sun was shining. I could hear birds chirping, small animals scampering about, and I thought I caught sight of a snake in a tree. It was either a snake or one of those willow type of branches that was swaying in the wind.

These trees looked similar to what we had back home on Earth, but they were bigger. Probably because we cut down our trees and never gave them very long to grow. I doubt these trees had ever been cut down.

A few of them looked like something out of *Swiss Family Robinson.* I suppose that if we didn't find any more of my people, they could easily create rather large tree houses in this section of the woods once we left. Until then, I hoped they stayed out of sight. Getting caught by us or the insectoids would be worse than trying to make a go of it in these woods.

I still wish I would have run after Paris let us out of the cells, but I was too dazed and confused to think straight. Once I did finally think about running, it was too late. The warriors had already found us.

The warriors up front with Lorlo cut a path for us. Then,

all of a sudden, Lorlo, who was in the lead put his right fist up, then the rest of the aliens stopped chatting and motioned for us to be quiet as well. Lorlo stopped and knelt down to look at the foliage on the ground. There looked to be vines crawling all throughout the small bushes. Now all of the warriors seemed alert and were looking around us and up into the trees.

I whispered to Zelan, "What's going on?"

"Shh, Lorlo has found signs of others coming through here," he whispered back so low, I could barely hear him. His lips were directly next to my ear, and I tried to stop the shiver that raced down my back, but I couldn't. Hopefully, Zelan was too busy paying attention to our surroundings to notice how much he affected me.

It wasn't like I was attracted to him. I think it had just been so long since a nice-looking man had touched me that my body reacted. That was all it was, or at least that was the story I was sticking with if anyone asked.

Lorlo stood up and motioned with his hand toward the right side. He held up three fingers and motioned three times to the right, like something out of a military movie. The warriors moved forward quietly, while those of us untrained in stealth, made a bunch of racket.

I stepped on a twig that broke, and I heard Lucy stomping on a small bush. There was no way we were going to sneak up on anyone. Still, I couldn't figure out why they thought bringing us would be a good idea.

As we moved through the jungle, I could no longer hear the birds or see any small animals. I thought about all the scary movies I had watched growing up. The girl who gets eaten by a monster, or killed by the crazy guy, always noticed how quiet it was before the psycho monster attacked. I kept alert looking around us as we moved very slowly towards the area Lorlo kept gesturing toward. Thankfully, I was mostly in the middle of the group, and Zelan was next to me as he promised.

I heard some rustling up ahead as I lost sight of those in the lead. Then I heard a phaser gun go off. In fact, I heard several phasers fire. My eyes grew wide, and I was about to scream when Zelan pushed me down on the damp earth. I turned my head toward the sound of the fighting and noticed that other warriors had tackled some of our women. My heart was beating out of my chest. Why were the warriors laying on top of the girls with their weapons drawn? What was going on in front of us? I tried to count how many were still in our party, but I couldn't turn my head far enough to see those behind me.

I watched as Lorlo came back and looked at everyone lying down, "Zelan, I need to show you something. The rest of you might want to back off a little." He turned around to go back to where he came from, and Zelan jumped up and started to walk away.

"Hey, I thought you weren't going to leave my side the entire time? You can't leave me here while there are still who knows how many bugs out there that might attack." I started to walk after him, then he turned around.

"Natalie, you are right. Be careful and stay close." He put out an arm out for me to grab, and when I did, we walked toward Lorlo. His firm face softened when he looked at me and it made me feel better.

As soon as we caught up to Lorlo and the other warriors, I almost puked. I wished that I would have stayed back where I was. Down on the ground were two women who had their heads blown off. But that wasn't the worst part. Inside where their brains should be were small cockroaches! They were covered in them.

I turned around and started to gag, and Zelan put his hand on my back. "Shh, it's alright. Natalie, there was nothing we could have done for them. Trust me when I say it is better that we killed them now."

"What happened? Why did they have so many cock-roaches on them? And what do you mean it's better you killed them now? Haven't they been dead a long time? How else did all those bugs get on them?" I blurted out as I tried to clean off my face.

Then I remembered a scene from *CSI* where one of the main guys, Grissom, said that bug infestations took at least 24 hours. With all those bugs on them, it must have been several days since they died.

"This is how the Insectoids reproduce. They infect a humanoid host with their offspring by inserting their repro-ductive gland inside the mouth and delivering a sack full of eggs. Once the host is infected… there is no cure other than death. If they stay alive, they will suffer a fate worse than death." He shook his head and took a deep breath.

"Once those bugs hatch, they eat their way out of the host's body. The host suffers more than you can imagine for hours before they finally die. This is why we checked you as soon as you had been attacked by that Zateelian. When I killed him, he may have sent his sack into your mouth. It is rare that it happens that way, but not unheard of." He held me tight to him and rubbed my back.

I pulled away and turned my head back to where we had come from.

His veins pulsed blue and I knew he was upset. But I did not know the cause of his angst. Could it be he was sad that humans had to die in this manner? Or was he upset because the Zateelians were procreating? Or, was it something else?

"Is that what the doctor meant when he said I was clean? Even though I was covered in goo?" I took a few deep breaths and tried to calm myself. I was very grateful that humans didn't have veins pulsing different colors to show our moods.

"Yes, he meant that your body was clean of any possible

parasites." Zelan grabbed me by the shoulders and pulled me close for a hug. Normally I would have pulled away, but today, I needed it more than I needed air.

"They were still alive when you guys found them?" I asked as I took several breaths and tried to keep from passing out or puking.

Lorlo walked over to us. "Yes, they were barely alive. The parasites had already started to eat their way out. I think we killed them all, but since they are so small, it is really difficult to say."

"What about the rest of the people who escaped? Do you think they have been infected as well?" A sinking feeling in the pit of stomach told me I didn't want to know the answer.

"It's hard to say. Some of them probably got far enough away before the Insectoids even got close to our ship. As long as they kept going, and didn't stop along the way, they should be fine. But I must warn you, there are other predators on this planet. Also, some of the vegetation might look edible, when in fact, it is poisonous. So, don't touch anything without asking one of us first." Lorlo left us and went back over to the bodies.

"Zelan, what do we do about those bodies now? We can't just leave them here out in the open for predators to come and eat. They need to be buried."

"Actually, we have to burn them. I am sorry, but it is required of all bodies that have been infested. We have no way to know that there aren't other parasites inside waiting to be hatched." He rubbed my back, and I realized I was still in his arms. Even though there were two dead bodies in front of me, I actually felt safe and protected.

"Can we leave yet? Or do you have to burn them now?" I pulled out of his arms and looked back in the direction of where the rest of our group was. It felt strange and nice being in his arms, which only confused me. This was not something I wanted to think about right now. Although, it was a nicer topic than the cockroach infested corpses in front of us.

"Due to the dense foliage, we have to stay here until their bodies are completely cremated. This could take a while. Why don't we go back to the group and explain to them what is going on? I don't want to split the team, so we all need to stay here together until the job is done." Zelan put his hand on my back and led me over to the other women.

"Do you see this often?" I wondered how often they encountered bodies like this.

"I have not seen it in a while. The fact that insectoids are this close to Earth is very worrisome. The Commander mentioned war. It is possible the insectoids are looking to take human hosts so they can reproduce more soldiers for the war. If that is the case, they were very stupid to bait us like this. Unless, hmm..." Zelan seemed to be talking more to himself than me. He mentioned some war tactics or something. I wasn't paying much attention.

The images of those women were seared into my brain, and I couldn't expunge that memory. Even though I was trying hard. What could get those images and smell out of my mind? It reminded me of one of those slasher movies- the kind with Jason or Freddie.

There was blood all over the place. The heads of those women were blown to bits. Small cockroaches, that also resembled grasshoppers, were everywhere. The smell was a cross between a garbage dump and burnt flesh. My nose was itching. I wished I had something better to smell.

When we made our way back to the group, Zelan had his arm around me and Rachelle made a stupid comment, "Looks like you're wasting no time grabbing a man, Natalie. What happened to that precious fiancé of yours back home?"

How did she know about Ben? "Rachelle, you have no clue what's going on, so just shut your trap." I was in no mood to deal with a petty, jealous girl.

She looked over to Zelan, who was looking at me. Then she put on a totally fake pout and brushed up against Telan. "Telan, why is she so mean to me? Especially when I have been nothing but nice to her." Rachelle rubbed her hands across his chest, and he looked to be caught in her trap.

I rolled my eyes, "Pa-lease! You are so obvious in your ways, Rachelle. Grow up and realize we're not in high school anymore. You know what? Come with me. I want to show you what we are dealing with." I walked over, grabbed her arm, and pulled her toward the area where the bodies were located.

Zelan ran up to me, "Natalie, you might not want to show her. It's pretty gruesome."

"I think she needs to know what we are up against here. Maybe then she'll stop her juvenile games if she understands the danger we're all in." In fact, I thought all the humans needed to know what was really going on.

Most of us had wanted to find a way to escape our captors. The planet seemed like an alright place to settle and re-build our lives. There wouldn't be any way we could steal a ship and go home. The realization was starting to sink in for all of us. But now, with this new threat, I was starting to think sticking close to Zelan and his friends was the smart move. Well, that is, until they killed all the Zateelians. Then maybe we could risk a jail break.

"Um, hello! Right here. No need to talk about me as though I'm somewhere else." She pointed to her chest. "What are you two talking about? We crashed, and you guys have killed all of the aliens who destroyed our ship, right?" She looked at Zelan and brushed her hand along his shoulder.

I shook my head and walked into the clearing that the warriors had made. They worked fast to clear an area so that they could burn the bodies without catching the plant life on fire in the process.

Once we stopped, I pointed to the bodies. "Look, do you see that?"

Rachelle, leaned over and squinted her eyes, "Eww, what is that? And that smell, gross." She covered her nose and mouth with her hand.

"That was two women who escaped our ship only to become incubators for the Zateelians." I crossed my arms over my chest and stood there watching her.

"Ha, ha. No really, what is it?" She screwed up her nose while taking a step closer. She looked back over her shoulder at me, "That is not a human being. Whatever it is, it's covered in cockroaches and other bugs. Is that some sort of dead animal?"

"Rachelle, this isn't a joke. Those insectoids infect a human host with their egg sacks and when the babies hatch, they eat their way out of the host body. That is what was happening when we came upon those bodies earlier." I raised one eyebrow at her.

"Gross! NO way!" She walked to the closest warrior, "Marcon, please tell me the truth about what happened here." She pointed to the mutilated bodies.

"I am sorry, Rachelle, Natalie told you the truth. This is what the bugs want humans for. Well, they use them for slaves until they are no longer useful, then they become food for their hatchlings." He went back to cleaning out the area of leftover bugs and foliage.

Rachelle's eyes bugged out as she realized I told her the truth. She turned around and ran screaming back to Telan. "Telan, you are not going to believe what I just saw ... and smelled!" She shivered and put herself up against his torso and wrapped her arms around him. He looked over to Zelan and shrugged his shoulders before putting his arms around the sniveling girl.

We spent the next couple of hours waiting for the bodies to be turned into ash. Almost everyone was fairly quiet once

Rachelle calmed down enough to relay her story. A few of the women eyed me wearily. It almost felt like they were upset with me for showing Rachelle the truth. Why they would be upset, I couldn't guess. I sat where I was and pondered my life today.

CHAPTER FIVE

I wasn't a religious person. However, I did think we should say something nice about the women who died today. Only one other person joined me, Lucy. "Lord, I know I don't talk much to you, but I would ask that these two women be received to your loving arms today. And if there are any more humans in the insectoid's hands, please make sure they don't end up like this." I waved to the funeral pyre. "Amen."

"Lucy, did you want to say something?" I asked.

"Yes. Dear Lord, none of us asked for this, but here we are. Please bring these two women to safety in your loving arms. I pray that they knew You before they died. And please don't let this happen to anyone else here on this planet or any planets. Will you please stop these insectoids from killing people like this? Amen." She wiped a tear from her eyes, then sniffed.

Telan spoke up, "Alright, we have a long way to go, and this seriously slowed us down. We might have to find a place and hunker down for the night. Since we are closer to the old ship, let's head that way."

"I agree. The Commander needs to be notified, but I can

do that while we walk," Zelan announced as he started for the ship.

"Wait, are we gonna stop looking for more humans?" I thought the main reason for this expedition was to look for survivors.

"For this trip, yes. If we stay the night in the damaged ship, we could look on our way back tomorrow. However, we will have some heavy equipment with us. It might be better to come out on a different day and just spend the time looking for anyone else." Zelan put his hand on my back, and we walked forward.

I used to hate it when Ben would put his hand on my back. He would put it between my shoulder blades and push. It was more like a shove, to get me to go where he wanted me. But, when Zelan did it, he put his hand in the small of my back and stepped closer to me. It was almost like a hug instead of a push. I never realized that it could feel nice to have a man's hand on my back.

It must have taken us at least an hour of hiking through the jungle to get to our old ship. Strange how I now associated what was once a prison as "our old ship." Did that mean I was accepting my fate?

"Lucy, how do you feel about the old ship versus the new ship?" I asked as we pushed aside some vines in our path, which were hanging from what looked like a banyan tree.

"What do you mean?" she asked as she threw one vine behind her and almost hit Rachelle with it. I looked back when I heard Rachelle squawk, and I almost laughed. The vine must have had some mud on it as there were splashes of it on her face.

I turned my head forward and had to put my hand over my mouth to cover my smile. It wasn't nice of me to laugh at Rachelle's situation, but I just couldn't help myself. Even though I was twenty-four, I still hadn't outgrown some of the high school silliness.

"Do you think back to the old ship fondly? Or is the new ship better? I guess I'm asking because I was just thinking about our situation and caught myself calling it *our ship*. How weird is that?" I shook my head as I stepped over some rocks.

"Huh, I guess I haven't really thought of it that way yet. Although, now that you mention it, I do miss the easiness of the last few days before the move to our new cells. Not that living in constant threat of bugs attacking is easy. More like, the freedom we had to move around our part of the ship. Maybe it was just that we weren't inside of cells anymore." She sighed and shook her head as she walked around the trunk of a banyan tree.

I followed her around, "Yea, maybe that was…" I stopped abruptly as Zelan pulled me down to the ground. Then I heard phaser fire.

"Zelan, what's going on?" I whispered to him.

"I hear the insectoids ahead. They have fired at our forward team. Can you use a Taser?" My eyes widened with horror.

"I…I have never used a gun of any sort. Not even a toy gun." I had always played with Barbie's and dolls. Growing up I played with girls, none of whom ever wanted to touch boy toys. I guess you could call me a girly-girl when I was a kid. Kinda wish I would have learned how to hold a weapon at the very least. But there was never a need to.

He scooted off me and pulled me behind the banyan tree we had just walked around. "Take this, you point it at your target and shoot. You will need to hold the trigger while you are shocking the enemy. But be careful, you only get one shot with this."

"When we get out of this, will you teach me how to use a phaser gun?" I was not going to be stuck with just a one-time-use, temporary weapon again.

"Yes, I think several of you will need to learn how to defend yourselves. Normally, we don't arm the slaves, but some of you are going to become mates. We need to make sure you can take care of yourselves." He moved to the side of the tree and took a defensive position.

He motioned for me to stay behind him. "Natalie, this is just in case a Zateelian gets past me. You should never have to fight. I am sorry I put you in this situation. We are so close to the ship too! Ghazem!" I wasn't sure what that last word meant, but I had a feeling it wasn't a nice word. I had never heard any of the aliens use human cuss words, but I had no clue if they swore in their own tongue.

Ben cussed up a storm, especially when he was drunk. I didn't like being around him when he was like that. I usually got into trouble. One time, we had been at his buddy's house watching a football game, and his team lost. It was stupid of me, I know, but I made a comment about sometimes they lose and sometimes they win. He got really mad and slapped me across the face. After that, I tried to get away from him when he drank.

A cold sweat poured down my back as the fighting came closer to us. I shouldn't have been thinking about other things while there were evil aliens about.

The warriors leading us raced back to where we were and took cover behind some trees near us. They fired their phaser guns from the sides of the trees, one guy even climbed up into a tree for a better angle. Zelan started firing, but I couldn't see the cockroaches yet. I craned my neck to look around the tree, and I still couldn't see them. I needed to find them before they found me.

"Watch out! They are scurrying along the ground and using the underbrush to hide," Marcon yelled as he fired at a bush that jiggled. When he hit it, I understood why. The bug's head exploded, and goo flew everywhere. But there were other bushes that kept moving and bristling closer to us.

Zelan got down on the ground, on his stomach, and fired

at the bushes that were moving. "The backside of their cara-
pace is too tough to penetrate with our handguns, but if you
can get low enough, then you might have a chance at hitting
them in the neck. Sometimes they will also have a sensitive
spot on their belly, but that is only the case when dealing
with younger bugs." He kept firing and hit one. The bush
stopped moving, and I saw a partial cockroach body move up
and then down again. Almost like a bowling pin that had
been hit hard from the bottom.

By this point, there were only a few remaining cockroaches. Or at least, only a few moving bushes. Another
warrior, Tosie I think was his name, got up into a tree close
to where a bush was shaking, and he jumped down on top of
it. I wished he hadn't done that. The bug wasn't alone.

While Tosie was battling the bug he jumped on, another
came behind him and used its hand-pincher. The bug used
his appendage as a sword and struck him through the chest.
Tosie's eyes flew open in shock, and he slumped down on the
ground. I muffled a scream as my eyes flew wide open.

I watched the whole scene play out, and it was the worst
thing I had ever seen. No, it was the second worst. The image
reminded me of the dead women with their blown-off, cockroach infested heads. I shuddered. This life wasn't for the
faint of heart.

I pushed myself back further behind the tree so I couldn't
see anything. This was not my area of expertise. If you had a
tax return that you needed audited, I was your girl. Fighting
with mutant cockroaches that looked like they had bred with
grasshoppers, not my thing.

Zelan seemed to be in his element. He moved around on
the ground while still on his belly shooting at anything that
made the bushes or vines wiggle. He focused on one spot and
shot it at least five times before it stopped moving. Then he
quickly moved around to another position and finished off
what appeared to be the last rustling bush.

Several of the surviving warriors went around and kicked the bodies of the bugs over and shot them in the face and chest before moving on to the next one. "Zelan, why are they doing that?" I asked as I watched in horror.

"It is to make sure they are really dead." He sighed and came over to hug me, but I wouldn't let him.

"Stop, I can't deal with anyone touching me right now. My skin is still crawling with the image of the bugs crawling all over the place." I shivered uncontrollably as I walked towards the other women.

Zelan walked into the center of our group, "We are going to return to the ship. This has turned into a very dangerous trip. Tomorrow I will bring a group of warriors back to the old ship and retrieve a few replicators. Until we eradicate the Zateelians on this planet, I don't want any more humans outside of the ship." A few of the women were grumbling, but I agreed with Zelan. It was too dangerous.

I raised my hand like I would have in college. "Are we going to be stuck in those cells again?"

He narrowed his eyes at me and said, "Yes, unless you are mated to a warrior, you are still a slave. I know none of you want that, so I suggest you find a warrior to mate with … soon." With that, he took off leading our group back to the new ship.

Lucy walked up beside me, "What happened? He looks to be very mad at you." She raised her eyebrows and looked up at Zelan.

"Yeah, I kind of offended him. He tried to hug me, and I pushed him away." I shrugged my shoulders and looked at the ground, I didn't want to look at Zelan.

It was a good thing too! Right in front of me were some small cockroaches. I jumped and screamed, "Cockroaches! Cockroaches!" Then pointed down on the ground.

The nearest warriors ran to me and pulled out their phaser guns and opened fire on them. I wasn't sure how many there were, but I couldn't get rid of the feeling that they were on me. I kept rubbing my arms and looking around to see if there were more than the five or six I think I saw.

Lorlo looked at me and smiled, "It's okay, we got them. They were most likely from the girls we saw earlier. I wouldn't be surprised if a few more got away before we killed them. We just need to be more careful about where we walk. Keep your eyes open." He patted me on the shoulder and took up his guard post again.

"Thanks, Lorlo." I shivered as I stepped over the dead carcasses. Thankfully they weren't any bigger. But I still kept rubbing my arms and occasionally looking at my legs, to make sure there weren't any on me.

We must have been walking faster than I realized because we made good time getting back, that or I was just stuck in my head.

On the trek back to the ship, I thought about Zelan. Mentally, I compared him to Ben. Other than being abducted, Zelan was a much better representation of what a man should be. He had proven himself to be a gentleman repeatedly by opening doors, making sure I was safe, and never once did he raise his voice, or his hand to me. I wondered if I could actually marry this man ... alien, whatever.

Zelan was a pureblood, so he looked a bit different from the VZ hybrids with a purple hue to his skin. His veins pulsed different colors. My emotions were affected by the various colors Zelan's veins pulsed, especially when they were purple. How weird was that?

Considering I had now seen two different alien species, I was surprised at how close the V'Zenians looked to us. It was no wonder they had chosen humans to be their mates. I wasn't a scientist, but I did wonder how close our DNA was to theirs and what that meant for us as a species. Could it be we were somehow created from the same interstellar ingredients?

The Zateelians were so different from humans and V'Zenians.

Just like the other women, Zelan's job bothered me. I think that would be the only thing to keep me from accepting him. I couldn't tolerate slavery. No matter how good-looking the alien was.

So there it was, he would only be a pseudo-friend.

If at all possible, I needed to speak with Paris. How could she mate with the leader of a slave trader group of aliens? That was just too weird. Especially since she was the one who originally wanted to find a way to mutiny and take the ship over and head it back home to Earth.

As we entered the ship, I could hear Rachelle flirting with Zelan, but he wasn't laughing. I heard her saying something about how she'd make him feel better. It was too much, so I pushed ahead further into the group. Normally, it wouldn't have bothered me. But he was just showing me what a gentleman he could be and as soon as I got upset, he let some woman flirt with him. She probably had her hands all over him too. Why did he let her touch him?

I put my hand over my mouth before I screamed. Realization dawned on me that I was jealous. Not. Cool. At. All. Why should I be jealous over that stupid chick? I was the one who pushed him away when all he wanted was a hug. I shouldn't have done that. He might have just needed a human touch.

There was no way I could be happy with his current job. If I married him and accompanied them to Earth, I would end up doing my best to stop them from taking women against their will. Somehow, I seriously doubted the Commander would be happy with me. Or, would it give me just the opportunity I needed to get home? Could I escape on the next trip to Earth? Maybe even warn my government about the V'Zenians and the Zateelians?

Did I want to go home?

Betty was standing next to me, and she complained, "Ugh, do we have to go back into those cells? Come on guys. After today, do you really think we would take a chance and leave the ship on our own?" She looked between Telan and Zelan.

"I am sorry, but you know the rules. Unless you agree to mate with a warrior who claims you as his true mate, you must stay in the holding cells." Telan looked over at Rachelle who was hanging all over Zelan.

Zelan kept trying to push her away, and she kept pawing him. It was as though she was an octopus. She must have had eight arms to be able to constantly be touching him all over when he kept moving her hands away from him. How could she be so obvious and forward?

Poor Telan, she dumped him before he even had a chance to get her attention. Oh well, he was better off without her. I think all the males on this ship would be better off without her. She was so fake with her affections and attentions. I wondered what she was up to.

Telan was walking past me when I stopped him, "Telan, is there a way to get a message to Paris? I really need to talk to her." Maybe she figured out a way to persuade the commander to free the slaves, or something. She just didn't seem like the type to marry an alien like that. Especially when she was the one who originally wanted us all to band together and take over the ship.

"I will see what I can do. The Commander keeps her close to his side at all times. Since I don't get invited to the bridge very often, I rarely see her." He shrugged his shoulders, which seemed like a very human response.

"Wait." I put my hand out to stop him from moving on. "Are you telling me Paris is still a prisoner? Even though they mated?" That couldn't be right. He promised her free reign of the ship if she mated with him.

"No, she isn't a prisoner. He thinks he is protecting her from the bugs. She got into a couple of fights with them, and the Commander doesn't want her injured again." He smiled and walked on, I let him go without another word.

CHAPTER SIX

We missed dinner being out on that adventure today. Thank goodness! So Zelan brought us all protein bars. While they weren't as good as the ones I ate back home, they were much better than the chalky jello mold. The consistency of the white stuff was more like dog food and one of the other women even said it smelled like the can of Pedigree she fed her dog back home. Which only served to make me hate the stuff even more.

"Thank you, Zelan. I appreciate this more than you know," I said quietly, as I took the food bar from behind the prison cell they locked us up in after we returned.

The protein bar tasted more like hard grains and grass, but anything was better than eating dog food.

"Sure thing. No problem," Zelan said as he walked away. I felt a stab of pain when he left. He wouldn't even look me in the eye. However, I saw enough of his face to know that he wasn't happy. His veins were pulsing a dark blue, his eyes were furrowed, and he had no smile. Normally, he smiled when he spoke with me. I missed his smile and the purple veins, and these feelings had me confused. But I couldn't give in. Not now.

About an hour later Paris showed up. I got excited when I saw her. I needed to talk to her about what had happened this morning, but more importantly, I needed to discuss my feelings for Zelan. They were becoming more intense, and I needed some answers. "Paris, it is good to see you. I take it Telan was able to get my message to you?" I grabbed ahold of the bars in front of me as she walked closer.

"Yes, I passed him on the way to the mess hall, and he told me you needed to see me tonight. What's up? Are you okay?" She looked me over and her brow furrowed when she noticed how dirty I was. They hadn't let us shower yet, so I can only imagine how bad I looked.

"Is there anywhere we can go somewhere to talk? I have some important questions. Questions that shouldn't be asked out in public like this." I waved to my surroundings. Talking about my feelings was going to be hard enough, but doing so with an audience? That would not happen.

She looked around the room and grabbed her lower lip with her teeth, "Yes, I think we can get an escort to my room. I'll see what we can do about getting you some clean clothes and a shower as well."

I sighed with relief, "Thank you so much, Paris." I smiled and backed into Lucy. There wasn't much room in here, and I needed to make sure the area in front of our cell door wasn't crowded or our jailers wouldn't open it.

Lorlo was the closest guard, and Paris had gestured for him to come over. "Hi there, Lorlo. Can you open this door? I need to take Natalie with me to my room." She pointed to me.

"Sure, but does the Commander know you are doing this? I don't want him coming down on me for letting a slave out if there isn't permission." The burly jailor furrowed his brow and stared at me. To be honest, he kind of scared me.

"She is not a slave! How many times do I have to tell you guys! Ugh, just let her out." Paris threw her hands in the air.

"I'll take full responsibility. We're going to my quarters, so the Commander will know, if he doesn't already." She pointed to the cameras on the wall nearest my cell.

I wondered if the Commander watched her every move on this ship via those cameras.

"Alright, have it your way. It's your head if he doesn't like this." Lorlo shook his head and unlocked my cell.

I walked out and was going to hug Paris, but she put up her hand, "No way. No hugs until you have showered." Then she waved her hand in front of her face and scrunched her nose. "Lorlo, you guys need to make sure the women are getting a chance to shower on a regular basis. Haven't you noticed how ripe it is in here?"

"Yes, well, um..." He nervously moved from foot to foot. "The Captain, he doesn't want the slav.... I mean, humans, to walk around the ship. He told us we had to keep them here."

"Are you planning on keeping them from showering for the next five months? You do realize they will get sick and could die from infections? Right?" The look she gave Lorlo could kill a lesser man, and he wasn't immune to it either. He backed up, licked his lips, and quickly blinked his eyes.

"I am just following orders, ma'am. If you can get the Commander to allow it, we would be happy to escort the humans to showers on a regular basis." Lorlo quickly locked the cell door. He stayed behind me, and out of Paris' line of sight. What a chicken.

"Come on, Natalie. Let's go get you cleaned up. Then we can chat about what's been going on lately." She led the way to her cabin in silence. A guard I didn't recognize followed us, and after about two or three steps, he increased the distance between us. I lifted up my right arm and smelled. Yup, I was ripe for the picking! Gross! Maybe Zelan wasn't upset with me after all. Instead, he was disgusted with how dirty I was.

We made it to her room and the guard stayed outside. She

didn't say anything to him, he just seemed to know his place. Strange. Once we were inside her quarters I asked her, "Who is that guard outside?"

"Oh, that's just Golen. He's one of my regular bodyguards." She gestured dismissively toward the door.

"Don't you mean jailor? Didn't you just change one cell for another one? Albeit, a nicer cell, but it still seems like you're a prisoner." My head swiveled around taking in the sight of the room. The living quarters were quite nice. There was a bedroom to one side, a living room in the middle, and a kitchen off to the other side. It was like a small apartment. Had I known about their living conditions, I might have been a bit nicer to Zelan.

"No, he really is here to protect me. I can go anywhere I want, and no one says anything. Well, unless I try to go outside. Venay doesn't want me anywhere near those insectoids. I don't blame him. They are pretty dangerous, and I'm still healing from when I first met them." She chuckled as she led me to the bathroom. It was located behind the kitchen.

"Why are you laughing? That seems like it would be awful, not funny." I stepped inside their bathroom. It was small compared to the ones back home. However, it was the largest I had seen on either space ship.

"Sorry, I was just remembering yesterday. I got turned around on this ship, and Venay was just walking with me. We were out for a stroll, so to speak. Anyway, I was leading and led us straight outside. He thought it was a ploy on my part to go somewhere. Not really sure where he thought I would go. However, he wasn't too happy with me. Instead of saying anything, he picked me up caveman style and threw me over his shoulder. He hightailed it back here, and when he put me down, the look on his face was priceless!" Instead of a chuckle, she was full on laughing now. She even bent over at the waist and held her stomach. I didn't see what was so funny.

The Commander walked into the area where we were standing, "It wasn't funny. I truly thought you were trying to run away. The Captain had been putting negative thoughts inside my head all day regarding the humans and how dangerous they were. He isn't a fan of mating with humans. He said he preferred to be single if his fated mate turned out to be a human." He sighed and kissed Paris on her forehead before heading back into the bedroom.

"I don't get it. What was the look that made you laugh?" I scratched my head as I looked between the two of them.

"He was so distraught. Instead of being mad, he looked like he was about to cry. His forehead was creased, and I could see the hurt in his eyes. I thought I even felt the sadness coming from him. When I explained that I was just turned around, his expression quickly changed, and he kissed me long and hard. We, well, never mind. But it was funny how he thought I wanted to run away from him, especially after the mating ceremony and the wonderful nights we've shared since then. There's no way I would leave him now. We have become bonded in a way I never thought possible." She smiled, pulled out two towels, and handed them to me.

"Thanks, but that still didn't seem very funny. At least not that funny. But I guess it was one of those, *you had to be there,* moments?" I took the towels, turned, and set them down on the cabinet inside the bathroom.

"Yea, probably. I'll never forget that pained look on his face. At least I know he never wants me to leave him. That's good." She turned to leave, then over her shoulder she said, "I'll bring in some clean clothes for you. I don't want you putting any of those clothes back on again." She plugged her nose letting me know I stunk. "Their washing machine probably won't be able to clean those so we might as well burn them."

"Okay, sure." I went inside and took one of the best

showers I'd ever had. I washed and conditioned my hair twice. That was probably overkill, but you never knew what yucky stuff made it back into the ship with me. The shower water ran quite dirty for the first seven or eight minutes. So, I didn't feel too bad about taking a fifteen-minute shower.

Once I was ready, Paris was in the living room waiting for me. She had set out a tea service with something that looked like it might be cookies. Since it was alien, I couldn't really tell. I sat down next to her on the couch.

"Here, try this tea." She handed me a cup of warm tea that smelled like a mix of peppermint and cinnamon.

"Hmmm, what is it? It smells wonderful!" I took a slow sip, and it was fabulous.

"They call it comfort tea. Or at least that's the closest translation. I've been drinking this since I made my way back to Venay when we were on the other ship. Maybe each night you can join me and some of the other mates for our evening tea. We're sorta making it a new tradition. I would have invited Lisa and Sheila tonight, but it sounded like you wanted to talk about something more than gossip. Am I right?" She took a sip of her tea and sighed.

"Yes, although I think I might like an evening of tea and gossip." I took a deep breath and decided to go for it. "Paris, how can you be married to a man who abducts humans for a living?" I put the tea down on the saucer in my lap and looked at her.

"I was wondering when I would be asked that question. However, I'm surprised it's you who's asking me first. Have you changed your mind about mating with a V'Zenian?" Paris arched an eyebrow.

"No, well, I don't know. There is one alien who has been paying me special attention. But I can't forget what they do and what happened to me. Although, I have come to realize that this really was a good thing for me. My fiancé was a horrible man. It took me until earlier today to realize this. At the same time, I realized that I'm too strong to let myself back into an unhealthy relationship." I took a sip from my tea and relaxed my shoulders.

"What makes you think that choosing a mate from those here on this ship would be unhealthy?" Paris picked up a cookie and took a bite. Then she tilted her head and really looked closely at me.

I squirmed in my seat with the scrutiny. "Choosing any alien who abducts people to use as slaves would be unhealthy. I thought you felt the same way? Which is why I'm here right now. How can you be okay with what the Commander does for a living?"

Paris took a deep breath, "I am not okay with what he's been doing for the past few years. But, I chose him because I am in love with him. Truly, I believe that I can help our people more by being right where I am. In time, an opportunity will present itself where I can change the status quo. If I'm elsewhere, say as a slave, I won't have an opportunity to do anything except cause a revolt on their planet. That won't help either side."

She made a good point. Being a slave wouldn't help my people in the long run. I needed to find a way to help them that also kept me safe so I could keep up the good fight.

"Will you accompany him on his next trip to Earth to grab more women and men?" I couldn't imagine accompanying Zelan back to Earth with the intent of abducting more people and forcing them to be slaves. I had come to realize that no one was going to force me to mate if I didn't want to, but my only other choice was to become a slave. It was a bad choice all the way around.

"Yes, they're gone for almost a year when everything goes as planned. I can't be away from my husband that long, it isn't healthy. Also, it might afford me an opportunity to change a few things. I have been discussing with him the possibility of taking longer to get the women, and even men. There are a couple of ideas in my head rolling around. We have discussed some of them, but I think we need to see what happens in the next year. You never know what their leaders might decide, especially since it looks like there will be war with the Zateelians." She picked up a cookie and offered it to me.

"Thanks, what are these?" I looked at it closely before taking a small, tentative bite.

"I don't really know what they are, but they remind me of madeleines. My favorite coffee house sold them. Once in a while when I had some extra change I would get one with my coffee. They were my second favorite treat." She smiled as she remembered her experiences.

"Paris, what happened to you? I heard you were homeless at a young age. Did your parents die?" She never did explain to any of us what happened.

She stood up and her hands shook. "Do you need any more tea? I have plenty and can make a fresh pot if you like? Or maybe a different kind of cookie?" She sniffed and wiped a tear away from her face.

"Sorry, let's talk about something else. Did you hear about my adventure today?" I said in a not so excited voice. It was anything but an adventure. Why those stupid aliens thought to bring a bunch of women along for that journey...I just couldn't believe it.

Paris inhaled sharply. "Yes, Venay was pretty upset with Zelan. After you found those women, you should have come back to the ship. I think that Zelan just wanted to spend time with you so badly that he wasn't thinking about the dangers for you. And now we have lost a warrior to the insectoids. Venay is very protective of his people. Losing a warrior has affected him, more than he wants to acknowledge." She took her seat again and leaned over the edge of the sofa and picked up a tissue.

It looked as though the aliens stocked up on some human

supplies. It made me wonder what else they picked up when they were on Earth.

"What about those women? They died such a horrible death. Did he think about them at all?" I knew that Tosie died a painful death, but at least it was quick. Those girls suffered for hours before we found them.

"Of course, he was heartbroken when he found out. At least he can visit with Tosie's family and tell them their son died with honor in battle. The families of those women will never know what happened to them. And the way they died..." Paris shivered. "Venay actually shuddered when Zelan told him. He told me it's one of the worst ways to die. Tomorrow he's sending out several search parties to see if he can recover any more of our people before the bugs get them." She shook her head and sighed.

"Do you think that anyone will willingly come back here? I don't think they would. If it was me, and I hadn't seen the insectoids yet, I wouldn't do it." I shook my head and prayed that any survivors would be alright.

"Same here. I think that's another reason why Zelan wanted a few of you along. So you could explain to the survivors why it is so important they come back willingly. Venay said it was too dangerous, so no more humans on the missions. At least, not until they have killed every single cockroach." I could hear the sadness in her voice when she spoke about the missing people. She out of all of us knows what's it's like to be out on the streets and all alone with no one to protect you.

Was she thinking about some of her experiences? Did this remind her of her old life? It was no wonder she accepted Venay so quickly. She knew what it was like to be all on your own with no one to lean on. No family to help in times of crisis.

I hadn't thought of her background before, at least not in

relation to her decision to marry her alien abductor. It was all starting to make sense.

I nodded my head in agreement. "That's smart. Do you think they'll get any replicators tomorrow? I don't know if I can take another day of that gross goop they call food we've been forced to eat." I almost gagged just thinking about it.

"I must admit, that was one of the biggest reasons why I accepted Venay's offer." She laughed and I followed suit. "He promised me real food, so I said yes."

I could believe that. If I hadn't just decided earlier today to stay out of unhealthy relationships, I might let Zelan claim me as his mate. Just so I could have better food, and a bed!

"I hope they do bring at least two back. Feeding our 'guests,' as Cazon affectionately calls them, is going to be difficult if we can't get them better food," she said.

"Yeah, but do you think we will be here for five months? Stuck in this ship?" The idea of staying here in jail cells for so long frightened me.

"Most likely. Venay said the other two ships that were fighting the insectoids in space left to get needed repairs from the closest space station they have. But they were not going home. Instead, they received new orders to patrol the border between the Zateelians and V'Zenians. I guess war is on the horizon, and they need more warships on the border. Venay isn't even sure if he will go back to Earth anytime soon. He might need to command a battle cruiser. His commanding officer, an Admiral Hosha'an, told him to stay here and help protect the settlement as well as this ship until reinforcements arrive." Paris's grip on her tea cup tightened and her knuckles turned white.

"Does that mean that you will be leaving us and going to the outpost?" I sat up straight and wondered how bad it would get if the Commander left the Captain in charge here. Something told me that would be very bad for us humans.

"Only for a few days. Venay wants to make sure their

defenses are up to snuff, and he also wants to take the shuttlecraft they have and see if he can find any more of our
people or the insectoids. We have to find everyone before the
re-supply ship arrives. Maybe if we can secure the planet,
then Venay will allow more freedom for all of you. Hopefully, me too." She pointed to her chest. "I know he means
well, but at times it does feel like I traded one jail cell for
another. Although, I do enjoy this one." She raised her
eyebrows in a suggestive manner, and I knew I did not want
to know any more details.

"Will you go with the Commander when he leaves?" I
didn't want her to leave us, she was the only one who could
help make our lives a little bit better.

"He won't leave me here. He said until we get to his home
world, he doesn't want me far from him. He feels safer that
way, and quite a few crew members have asked that I not
fight him on this. Apparently, when I'm not around he's a
real bear to deal with. Even the doctor asked me to stick
close to Venay." She chuckled.

"Yikes! Alright." I nodded thinking how I could use this to
my advantage. "Can I go with you? Do you think you could
find a reason to take me along? Paris, you've seen the cells
here. It's so packed that we can barely move around in there.
Maybe take a few women with you." Anything would be
better than staying in those cells packed like sardines.

"What reason do I give? I'm not going to suggest they stay
as slaves here on this planet. I'm still hoping to get them
freed by the time we get back to their home world." She
stood up and began pacing the floor in front of the sofa.

"I don't know. Maybe you could say some of them want
to see if their mates are in the settlement? Would the
Commander buy that excuse?" I asked.

She tapped her forefinger to her lips, put her thumb
under her chin, and "hmm'd" for a while. "That might work.
But I think Venay knows who your fated mate is. Although, if

we could get Zelan to go with us, then it would make sense to bring you. That would be an easier sell. I'll talk to him tonight about it and see if I can finagle a few more women too."

"I can hear you even with the door closed, you do realize that don't you?" Venay said as he walked out into the living room.

"Were you eavesdropping on our conversation?" Paris put her hands on her hips and pursed her lips.

"As soon as you said, 'gossip,' I tried very hard not to listen. But, I just heard you mentioning my name, so my ears perked up." He leaned over and kissed her on the cheek. Then sat down on a chair next to the sofa.

"So, Natalie, you want to go to the outpost with us? Why?" Venay looked at me and I quaked a bit in my boots, so to speak. He was very imposing. Even sitting down, he still towered over me. He didn't pulse blue or purple, he was pulsing orange and yellow. Didn't orange mean frustration? I hoped he wasn't frustrated with me.

"Well, I'll be honest. Those cells are so tight we can't even sit down in them. We're packed in there like sardines. I had to ask to see Paris in order to get a shower. Since we arrived on this ship, no showers have been granted to any of us." I tried looking him in the eyes, but I couldn't. He made me nervous. How did Paris deal with him? Surely, he always got his way with her. Maybe that's why she married him? He strong-armed her into it?

"I have not been down to the cells yet. First thing tomorrow I will take a look. However, I will make sure that everyone gets a shower on a regular basis. There is no excuse for not keeping you all clean. If the doctor knew this, he would be livid." He stood up and went back to the other room, but stopped just short of the door, "Natalie, if I were you, I wouldn't keep Zelan waiting too much longer. I have heard the gossip about him and some other woman. Zelan wants a mate. If you care for him, you will find a way to accept what he does. Paris has accepted what I do. Maybe she can help you." Then he walked into his room.

Paris put her finger to her lips and whispered, "Shh, if he can hear, you don't want to say anything negative right now. Just nod and go along with him. We'll get things changed, but it's easier to do so from within than it is as a slave."

"You're right," I whispered.

"How do you all sleep if you can't sit down?" Paris tilted her head and furrowed her brow.

"A few can sit at a time. They sleep sitting, and we take turns. It sucks, but it's the only way. I'm really tired. Do you think I could sleep on your couch tonight?" I felt the cushions on the sofa and realized it would be quite comfortable. And it would be the first time in days that I could lay flat without touching someone else.

"Sure, I don't see why not. You're going to need a good night's sleep if you go with us tomorrow to the settlement. I think Venay wants to leave mid-morning. But I should warn you, he gets up early and will come through here to get his breakfast before heading out. You'll most likely get woken up. Once he's gone, you can go back to sleep." She picked up her tea cup and took another sip.

"Thanks, Paris. You're a lifesaver! I truly don't know what any of us would do if you hadn't accepted his offer." I pointed to the closed door the Commander had gone through just a few minutes earlier.

"I do love him. At first, it wasn't about love. In the beginning, I accepted his offer as a ruse. I thought I could find a way off his ship or get it turned around and head back to Earth. Once I finally realized that wasn't going to happen … my feelings started to change. There's something to that mating bond everyone has been talking about. Do you feel it for Zelan?" She took another larger drink of her tea now that it was cooling down.

"I ... well, I don't think so. He's good looking and very nice. Zelan has proved to be a gentleman, well, aside from abducting innocent women. The past few days have been nice, or as nice as they can be when you're attacked by mutant cockroaches." A wry smile crossed my face.

"He does seem nice. I think you could do much worse than him. What about your fiancé back home? Are you over losing him yet?" Paris continued to whisper.

I chuckled. "I haven't missed Ben for several days now. In fact, I don't know that I ever loved him. He hit me once when he was drunk. Of course, he apologized the next day when he was sober and noticed the red welt on my cheek, but after that, my feelings for him changed. Even though this is not the best place to be, it might actually be a good thing I was abducted. I would never have left him. My family wouldn't have allowed it. Father introduced us when we were teenagers. It was expected that I would eventually marry Ben." I shook my head.

"This experience has taught me that I do love my family and miss them very much. Ben...not so much. I recently realized we had an unhealthy relationship, and I'm actually glad to be out of it. One day I do hope to marry and have kids, but it needs to be in a healthy, loving relationship. Not because I think my life will be easier. That was what it would have been with Ben, the easy way out. My father drilled into me from high school that I was to marry Ben after college. I love my dad, but he never saw the evil in Ben. Even I didn't realize how bad our relationship was until now. Ben was charismatic and everyone seemed to love him. He was good at putting on an angelic face." I looked down at my lap and felt a sting behind my eyes.

"I can understand that. It's good you realized that your relationship was toxic. Shoot, even I knew that after the first time we met. You told us several things about Ben that made me happy he was no longer in your life. What kind of man tells his fiancé she looks fat, when in fact she's very skinny? Or doesn't give her praise of any kind? Had you stayed with him, you would have ended up with an eating disorder." She handed me another cookie.

I gladly accepted it and thought *screw you Ben*! It actually felt good to not worry about what I ate for a change. During the past year, Ben had been trying to control my diet. He would have thrown a fit if he knew I was eating a cookie.

A smile crossed my face and I was happy, for a change.

Paris continued, "Zelan is a good guy maybe you just need time to get to know him better. And as for the slavery issue, being on the inside has already helped out a lot. They have never given their slaves anything more than that chalky stuff they fed us. So, while it isn't freedom, at least you all are getting better food and treated more humanely too. I think in the past, it was the doctor who insisted on regular showers, not the Commander." She quirked one eyebrow.

I thought about that. Maybe she was creating change. Even if it was slow, things were changing. I got the impression that none of the warriors called us anything other than slaves or mates before this trip. Now they are calling us humans, women, men, and sometimes guests. Hopefully, they will start seeing us in a better light and our treatment will be commensurate with their view of us.

"Thank you for all of the help you gave us. After the crash, it did seem as if we were on a more equal level. At least until we arrived here. Now we're back to being slaves and prisoners." I sighed and slouched. Exhaustion was overtaking me, and I had no more fight left in me for the day.

"Let's get some sleep and see what happens tomorrow. Maybe Venay will see the cells and order that you guys get better accommodations. Positive thinking usually helps me get some sleep too." She got up, brought me a pillow and blanket, and then gave me a hug goodnight. I was starting to think I might have a real friend in Paris.

CHAPTER SEVEN

The next morning brought with it a new sense of dread. Zelan came to Paris's door before I was up. He was to escort me the entire time we were away. Basically, I was his prisoner until we returned. Oh, joy. Not!

He walked in and moved my legs off the couch to sit next to me. "Good morning, Natalie. I understand that you wanted to go see the outpost today. Can I ask why?" He finally looked at me when he asked his question.

When he first sat down, he had looked straight ahead. His veins were pulsing between orange, blue, and yellow. Where was the purple? His eyes were always purple, and they were beautiful. But it was his veins that I enjoyed watching.

I must be going crazy.

"I needed to get out of those cells. We're too cramped in there. Plus, this is supposed to be a safe trip. The Commander wouldn't take Paris if there was going to be any danger, right?" I wiped the sleep from my eyes and yawned.

He pulsed black for a quick second, then a deep blue. "So, it had nothing to do with me? You didn't want to spend some time getting to know me better?"

His eyes held no trace of their normal spark, and he

pulsed a sky blue then navy blue. The black was gone, or maybe it was my imagination. He sighed and started to stand up.

"Wait. Yes, I did want to see you, too. Paris told me I should spend some time getting to know you better. She said that just because you take part in the abductions of hundreds of humans, it doesn't make you a bad guy. However, I do think that it makes you a bad guy." I looked over at him, and he had sadness written all over his face.

His eyes were closed. He hung his head and was very quiet. "I can understand why you would think that. Kidnapping women and even men isn't something I enjoy. You do know that my people are dying out, don't you?" He looked up at me with quivering lips and sad eyes.

"If we didn't find your people, mine would have died out by now. You probably don't understand, but most of us have trouble with this. We do it to save our race. My kind over the years have learned that this is how it is. We have to take humans to keep our species alive and kicking. Your planet is overrun with too many people who don't even appreciate what they have. One day, maybe you will understand and not judge me too harshly." He stood up, and I let him walk outside.

It was time to get up and get ready, but there was a lump in my throat and my heart hurt for the guy.

He was so sad and looked really lonely even though he was surrounded by his friends and fellow warriors. What must it be like to know that your entire civilization was on the brink of destruction? How would the leaders of my own planet act if we were in such a situation? Maybe it wasn't so cut and dry, but they needed to find another means of stabilizing their world.

As I prepared for the day, my heart was aching. I did understand to a certain degree where he was coming from, but I couldn't accept a husband who enslaved others. Maybe we could be friends. That was really all I could offer him at this point.

The Commander called us when the transport ship from the settlement arrived. I was actually excited to go with them on this trip. Sadly, I was the only *slave* allowed to go. Which meant that I would be spending a lot of time with Zelan. It might be ok, as long as he didn't push things. I needed to find an opportunity to tell him that we could be friends. Would that sound as bad to an alien as it would to a human?

Telan, Marcon, and Lorlo were also going with us. At least, I knew most of the aliens on this trip. The settlement sent two pilots with the ship, which made nine of us on this merry adventure. I really was merry, too. It was my first chance to meet aliens who lived with humans on a daily basis.

Paris said this would give us an idea of what it might be like for us on V'Zenia.

The pilot introduced himself to me as Haver, and his co-pilot was Aysiaer. Both were half human and half V'Zenian, or hybrids as they referred to themselves, and happy to see us. "Commander, it is so good to see more of my people here. I am truly sorry for the reason behind it. However, we are all very excited to have company. The outpost is quite small, and we have very few opportunities to meet new people." He smiled at Paris and me.

Aysiaer walked up to me and reached out to shake my hand as he introduced himself, but at the last minute, he kissed the top of my hand instead. "It is a pleasure to meet you, Natalie." He gave me a very rakish smile. This alien was going to be trouble. His veins pulsed red, I had seen that color, but very rarely, and I didn't know yet what it meant. Paris giggled, and Zelan put his arm around my shoulder like he was claiming me.

"Come on Natalie. Let's go and get buckled in before

take-off." Zelan was pulsing orange as we walked into the shuttle.

"What's wrong," I whispered to him.

He looked around and whispered back, "Stay away from Aysiaer. He looks like he will be trouble." Yup, he was jealous. It was kinda cute but also a little annoying. I didn't need guys fighting over me or even wanting me. For now, I was very content with being single for a change.

"Look, I'm not interested in anyone right now. You and I need to have a talk, and soon. I'm single for the first time in years, and I am not going to jump right into another relationship. Not now." I sat down next to him only because he was my chaperone for the trip. Well, and I didn't know how to fasten those belts. He fastened me in before the rest even made it on the ship.

The pilot and co-pilot went straight to their spots without even looking at me. Which was a relief.

It felt really strange as we took off. I didn't remember what it was like in the Commander's ship. I woke up in the prison cells after we had already taken off. Or did they use transporters? Strange, I never thought to ask.

The ship was loud, and it vibrated and shook as we moved up. From my vantage point, it appeared we went straight up in a line. When we hit our cruising altitude, we flew forward. Once we were moving forward, the ride was pretty smooth and not nearly as loud either.

I could see the tops of trees as we headed to the outpost. This was going to be very exciting, as long as Zelan realized we could only be friends.

"Zelan, how long is the flight?" I was enjoying this, and the view outside was incredible, but I had no idea how long we were going to be inside the craft.

"It shouldn't take more than two hours to get there. If we walked, it could take several days depending on how slowly we had to go."

"Do you think the insectoids have made it this far?" I had been looking forward, at the viewscreen, so I could see everything we were flying over.

He hesitated, and I looked at him. "They sent some of their troops over to the outpost. I heard the warriors did have to defend against a small attack. It seems they knew the exact location of the settlement, which tells me that they have been watching Zelaron 10 for quite some time."

"Zelaron 10? Is that the name of the settlement?" I asked.

"No, that is the planet. I think they call their settlement, New Hope."

"New Hope? That's an interesting name for an outpost that is five months from your home planet." I couldn't take my eyes off the viewscreen. The rich and vibrant greens of the forest we flew over were very enticing. It reminded me of fae books I had read when I was in high school. The colors were so different from the trees back home. I felt like I had ended up in faerie or someplace like that. If I wasn't so set on going home, I might like to stay here.

"I think it has to do with being so close to Earth. The leader of the outpost mated with a human. She may have named the place." He shrugged his shoulders.

"Was it just the one attack?" I almost whispered, as I thought about what it might be like to be in their settlement and be attacked by those mutant creatures.

"As far as I know, yes. We can ask them when we land. Are you nervous?" he put his hand on my leg and squeezed. It felt comforting so I let him keep his hand there.

"A little bit. I don't want to be attacked again by those bugs. They really freak me out. But I don't want to hide inside of the spaceship either." Part of me was being a chicken and I knew it. But another part of me wanted to stand up for myself and be strong. There was no way a weak person would be able to survive this planet. I would have to learn how to be more like Paris. She never seemed to be frightened and she certainly didn't back down.

"That's good. It isn't healthy to hide from your fears. You need to tackle them head on."

I smiled and thanked him for the pep talk. We kept quiet for the rest of the trip. It was a very companionable silence.

Once the outpost came into view, I got excited. The walls were made of some sort of metallic material that shined in the sunlight. There were parapets on all corners, and inside of them there were manned artillery guns. This settlement was more the size of a small city. They must have worked for years to create such a beautiful and safe place to live.

The walls had to be at least 25 feet high, and there were large gates on each side as well. They were all closed. We flew above the walls and into one side of the city that housed their maintenance bays. There were large metallic warehouses all along the side where we were headed. Two had artillery posts on top of them as well, but no one manned those at that moment. They must have been used in case of an aerial attack.

On the other side, I could see what looked like office buildings. They were four stories high and made of glass. It was the same material as the rest of the buildings and fences. I didn't notice any houses, though. So those offices might actually be apartments or condos. There were trees interspersed amongst the buildings, but other than those trees, there wasn't much color here. The buildings were all silver and glass. There wasn't any color on them.

Once we stopped moving forward, we went down. It felt almost like an elevator going very fast. Like the elevator in the Empire State Building. I went there once with my family when I was in high school. The elevators moved so quickly my ears popped. It was a smooth ride, and almost as exciting as a roller coaster.

One year later, I was told that I was expected to marry

Ben after college. From then on, we always vacationed together. His family never went anywhere without ours and vice versa. It was odd that we all spent so much time together, but my father was in business with Ben's father. They must have wanted to keep the business in the families, and that was why we were expected to marry. I guess my dad will just have to wait for my sister to finish college.

Now that I thought about it, she may have had a crush on Ben this whole time. I never really cared that she did. I guess distance really does help put things into perspective.

My hands fumbled on the straps as I was too excited to get them off so I could go outside and look around.

Zelan laughed as he took them off for me. "You sound like a kid who is going to her first gtocheen."

"Um, I don't have a universal translator yet. What was that you said?" I asked.

"We need to get you one. Maybe as soon as we get back you can get one? All the women should start working on getting them. It will be much simpler if you do. A gtocheen is a park we take our kids to. They can play around with other kids and also go on rides. They have many different rides for different ages of kids. Even adults enjoy them." He finally gave me a real smile. He must have been thinking of times he went with his family as a kid.

"That sounds like an amusement park. Back on Earth, we have lots of amusement parks all over the world. I can't wait to see what yours look like." I beamed from ear to ear thinking about riding alien roller coasters and 4D motion rides.

Zelan smiled and gave me a hug. "When we get home, I will take you to our biggest park. You will love it."

I was so excited I didn't even realize I had just let him hold me and make future plans for us until we were walking down the ramp holding hands. In order to keep from upsetting him again, I gently pulled my hand away so that I could point to something and ask what it was.

"Is that a warehouse or a business of some sort? Do they even have businesses here?" I pointed to a large building made from that shiny silver material.

"Yes, they have a few businesses here, but it is very different from Earth. They don't make goods to sell. They make what they need to survive as well as what we might need when we stop to pick up goods or make deliveries." We turned a corner and went deeper into the industrialized section.

"Usually, we stop here on our way to Earth and drop off a cargo hold full of supplies for them. On our way back we will stop for fresh food and water. They have their own fields here where they grow a lot of various fruits and vegetables in addition to the animals they raise."

"Wow, this sounds like a really cool place. Will we get a tour?" I walked around with my attention on what was in front of me, head raised, and mouth open in awe.

I walked right into Aysiaer. "Oh, sorry about that. I was too busy looking up." I quickly walked past him so as not to invite any conversation.

CHAPTER EIGHT

A very tall man and woman walked out of what looked to be an office on the side of the landing pad we were on. "Commander Venay, it is good to see you again. I was very sorry to hear your ship was broken up in the crash. We have plenty of space here if your crew would like to stay with us. We even have fairly comfortable accommodations for your slaves. Much better than the prisons you keep them in on your ships." He smiled as he looked at Paris and me.

"Thank you, Commander Croso. It is good to see you again. I am relieved that you were able to quickly deal with the Insectoids when they attacked you. I hope that our warriors can eradicate this planet of the bugs within a few days. Captain Mypo, may I introduce my mate, Paris." He motioned for Paris, and she walked up to his side and smiled at the two officers.

The Commander was an imposing man who stood almost seven feet tall. He was a hybrid, like Venay. Where all aliens good-looking? Was it something in their genetic make-up? His violet eyes and dark brown hair added to his good looks. He also had a warrior's build. His shoulders looked like that of a football player. They must have had wide doors in all of their buildings to allow for these large males to walk through.

The hard angles of his face told me he was tough, but his smile and the crinkles around his eyes gave him a softer look that made me think he had heart.

"Commander, Captain, it is nice to meet you both. I love your outpost so far. Would it be possible to get a tour of the city? This is much bigger than what I was expecting. When Venay said it was a settlement, I was thinking of something from Earth. Maybe even wooden fences." They all laughed.

Croso smiled and told Venay, "I like her." Then he looked at me, "Yes, I would love to take you and your friend on a tour of our village. Sadly, I need to discuss a few things with Venay. Maybe the Captain would like to take you all around?" He looked over at her, and she nodded her head.

The Captain held herself very stiffly, like she was at some formal event or something. Maybe Commander Venay intimidated to her too. He seemed to frighten everyone, except for Paris.

Captain Mypo looked to Commander Venay, "Commander, will your guards be escorting your mate and her slave? Or should I provide warriors?"

That ticked me off! I was no one's slave! I knew my face reflected my emotions because Paris took my hand and whispered to me, "Not now. Let's get through this first."

Zelan must not have liked it either, "Excuse me Captain, but Natalie is not a slave. She is my future mate." He stood next to me and put his hand on my shoulder.

I looked up to him and smiled. Even though I didn't like the idea of him claiming me as such, it would be nice to be treated decently while we were here.

Commander Venay looked at me with an arched eyebrow but didn't say anything.

"While we are here, I will be escorting her everywhere we

go. You won't need to worry about her." Zelan said as he squeezed my shoulder.

The Captain's look changed from a scowl to a smile with this announcement. She must not have liked the idea of a slave running around without supervision. Funny how once my status as a "mate" was confirmed it became fine. I have always hated segregation and discrimination. To see its manifestation here based on status instead of race, religion, or sexual orientation didn't lessen my disgust. This was going to be an enlightening visit. I hoped we were able to see the local "slaves" and how they were treated here.

"Follow me, and we can begin our tour." Mypo signaled for us to follow her, and the three of us did.

Captain Mypo was tall, but not quite as tall as the male warriors. She had to be close to six feet five inches. I wasn't exactly sure. She had long dark brown hair with waves and she was a purebred alien. She was the first female alien I had seen. Zelan told me their women chose to stay home and take care of their children and households. How was it that the outpost had such a high-ranking female warrior?

Would I meet more female warriors here at the outpost? I hoped so.

Both the Commander and the Captain wore the same type of military garb as Venay and Zelan. They had black camo pants with tight pockets on the side. Their shirts were button up and black as well. Their rank showed on their collars, but I hadn't yet learned what all they meant. Even though Croso and Venay were both Commanders, they looked to have different types of rank. Maybe they were in different branches of service?

Could the little stars on Venay's collar mean he was in some sort of air force? Croso and Mypo both had little eagles on their collars. Did that mean an army of some sort? Croso had four eagles and Mypo had three. Which seemed to mean their level of rank.

Mypo wasn't a very good tour guide. Most of what she told us was how things were built and who did what. We stayed mostly in the industrialized part of town.

"Excuse me, Captain Mypo, will you show us the areas of town where everyone lives? I am especially interested in how you treat your humans." I just couldn't call them slaves. That term was starting to really grate on my nerves. Everyone had been using it way too much lately. The new warriors from Captain Montgomery's ship had trouble calling us "humans," even though Commander Venay's crew had started using the term.

"Of course, we just have one stop to make on our way to the residential section." She turned her back and took us in the direction of what looked like the office complex.

"I thought you might appreciate seeing our newest buildings. These were designed by a group of our…humans, who live and work here in New Hope." She sounded like she almost choked when she said humans. I swear she had to clear her throat after using that word.

"Captain, you have humans who work in offices? What type of jobs do they hold?" Now I was curious. This could be a good thing for humanity as a whole. Paris had some interesting ideas about working with the leaders of Earth. Maybe they could send some of our people here to work. We certainly have a lot of office workers who are currently not working, maybe this could be the answer to some of our unemployment issues.

"I imagine they do similar work here as they did back on Earth. We have secretaries, receptionists, even a few managers who are all human. I think most work in supply and acquisition positions." She opened the glass door to a four-story building I had noticed on our way in today.

Inside looked just like office buildings back home. Tile floors, plants, although these looked real and not plastic, there were even some chairs, a sofa, and a table that housed some magazines. If I didn't know I was on an alien planet, I would have sworn I was home on Earth. Although, the walls were made of that strange metal. It was a cross between glass and metal. It was almost translucent. It was as thin as sheet metal, but seemed much stronger. I touched the wall and pushed on it a little bit and it didn't move at all. It didn't even buckle under the pressure from my hand. That was the only thing that made me think alien. Even the receptionist was human.

"Clarissa, I have some guests with us today and will be taking them on a tour. Are there any areas we should avoid today?" The Captain asked the young lady manning the desk.

She stood up. "No Captain, the leadership is all out meeting with Commander Venay, I believe. None have returned yet." She looked over to us and asked, "Would you like something to drink? We have coffee, tea, and bottled water. All of it from Earth." Her smile was very pleasant and inviting. Strange, she acted as though she was just a regular human doing a normal job. I would have expected her to cower before the Captain or even Zelan. But she seemed comfortable.

Paris walked up to her and shook her hand. "Hi, I'm Paris. This is my friend Natalie and her mate Zelan. I would love a coffee, if you have some ready, with milk and sugar. Is that possible? I haven't had any coffee in a while. Do you have flavored syrups too?"

Clarissa laughed and said, "Sorry, we only have regular coffee. But we do have cream and sugar. Why don't you all come with me, and I can show you our coffee corner."

Paris and I followed her while Zelan and the Captain followed us. "Paris, can you believe this? Real coffee! I thought I would never see this again! I can't wait. Although, I do wish they had hazelnut creamer. That would make this perfect." I almost did a happy dance I was so excited.

"I know what you mean, I wish they had peppermint

creamer. But any coffee would be a treat for me. Venay must stock them with coffee and everything from Earth. Maybe I can talk him into picking up some of our favorites next time he goes to Earth!" We both giggled while walking to the coffee corner.

When the reality hit me about what I was laughing about, I instantly felt guilty for getting excited about Commander Venay going back to Earth to pick up supplies. It would also mean he was abducting more people.

Their coffee corner was more like a coffee room. I would have called it a break room. It had to be at least 30' X 60'. There were tables and chairs in the middle of the room. On one side there were three refrigerators and a couple of cabinets. Another wall was entirely encompassed by a counter which featured a sink, three microwaves, and cabinets above and below. Whoever designed this room did it for humans.

There were even several big screen TV's up on the walls. They were playing different movies, human movies. My eyes were wide open as I turned around and looked at everything in the room. I felt like I was home. This was where I belonged.

Zelan walked up to me and took my hand, "Do you like this place?"

"I love it! I feel like I'm back on Earth."

Clarissa handed me a mug of coffee. "That's because a couple of our residents used to be architects back on Earth. They have designed several office buildings here and a few of their plans have even been shared with the homeworld. They're making quite the name for themselves." She beamed and looked to be quite proud of their accomplishments, as she should.

Paris went to add more sugar to her coffee. "You're residents here? Not slaves?" She looked at Clarissa, who looked to the Captain.

"Go ahead and tell her. I think they might like this part,"

the Captain said. She smiled her first real smile and relaxed just a bit.

"A couple of years ago there was a revolt by the slaves, and we almost got away. But, Commander Croso made a deal with all of us. If we worked for them, like we did for our employers back home, we could be considered residents instead of slaves. He wanted us to work together to make this a better outpost." Clarissa stirred her coffee and took a sip of the steaming nectar of the gods.

I was shocked. They had revolted and turned things around. This gave me hope for creating change once we made it to the homeworld. My mind was starting to think up new ideas and ways to change things for us.

Clarissa continued, "I think we did a really great job in the past few years. There are some more improvements in the works, but nothing like the office buildings. Back home, I was a receptionist for a big office building in downtown Denver. I really liked my job too. So, when we started talking about what we all used to do back on Earth, the leadership here decided that they could use some of those roles." Clarissa shrugged her shoulders.

Paris interrupted her, "Did many die in your revolt?"

"No, actually. It was a very short-lived battle. Well, maybe battle is too strong of a term. The Commander was mated to a human. She left him and joined us. When most of us escaped from the compound, the Commander and the Captain came after us with troops. Most of whom had already mated with humans. It was more like a discussion and negotiation." Clarissa would probably be a great person to speak with about ways to change things for good.

The Captain grabbed some water and took a seat near us.

"When we got back, we had to find a way to make it work. They needed roles filled and we were the best choice since we had the experience that the V'Zenians didn't have. Most of them were warriors or kids. So, it was a new thing for them to have to run a colony and any businesses needed here to keep things going." Clarissa explained.

"There is even a pizza joint and an ice cream parlor near the residential areas. You should come join us tonight. We have a BBQ planned with live music. Most of us are settling in now. We know that we can't go home. Lately, we have been creating things and places that remind us of home. Most of the VZ's," Clarissa put her hand out. "We call the aliens VZ's, like the improvements we have made. Some aren't a fan of ice cream, which just means more for us!" Clarissa announced cheerily.

"Do the leaders on the homeworld know that you have made all of these changes?" I asked. Paris and I had talked a little bit about making changes I wondered if it wouldn't be that difficult after all.

The Captain joined the conversation at that point, "No, and they don't need to know do they?" She raised one eyebrow as she looked at me.

"I won't say anything, but why not let them know about your advances? Especially since things are going so well here, and the homeworld likes the architectural changes. It seems to me that you have made happier humans who are now giving back a lot more than a slave would." I looked over to Clarissa "Isn't that right? None of this would have been possible with slaves."

Clarissa hemmed and hawed as she looked everywhere but at me. "Um…well, the leadership believes that if a slave doesn't perform then they can just be replaced. They don't care too much about making us humans happy, even if it does mean that we are more productive."

"Ah, I see. Alright, I won't say anything once we get to the homeworld." I looked over to Zelan. Maybe it wasn't going to be easy to make the necessary changes on V'Zenia after all.

"I won't say anything either, but I must tell you, I love what you are doing here. On the Commander's ship, we usually refer to the slaves as *humans* or lately as *guests*. None of us are comfortable with the term *slave*. I can't speak for the Commander but now that he has taken a human for his mate…" He shrugged his shoulders and looked at Paris.

"Yes, things are changing on Venay's ship. What I want to see is all of us working with the government back home and get volunteers instead of abductees. But it won't work until your," Paris pointed at the Captain, "government treats humans with more decency and respect. That is something I would like to work on. It's too bad we can't show them how wonderfully this outpost is run now."

"Commander Croso did try to feel out our leaders when he sent them the new office building plans and told them he wanted to staff it with more humans. They were not very receptive to having more humans work here. Especially since they had heard about our uprising five years ago." The Captain put her drink in the sink and waved for us to follow her.

We spent the next hour touring the building and watching as the humans and aliens interacted just like any two groups of people who worked together would. This gave me hope. Hope that one day soon, humans would get their freedom.

CHAPTER NINE

The Captain brought us to their guest quarters. I wasn't uncomfortable with Zelan at all today, until we were assigned our rooms. Since we were supposed to be mates, we had to sleep together. We weren't a real couple, and I was very nervous he would expect something from me. No one told me we were staying the night, or I would have said something sooner about wanting my own room.

Once we were in our room I asked Zelan, "Um, how is this going to work?"

"Don't worry, I will sleep on the floor. You can have the bed. I only told them you were my mate so that you wouldn't be treated like a slave today. Had I known they were forward thinkers, I wouldn't have said anything. If this is too uncomfortable for you, let me know and I will come clean." He scratched his head while looking at me and quirked the left side of his lips up.

"No, it's fine. I knew why you did it, and I am thankful to you for looking out for me. I don't like the idea of you sleeping on the floor though. If you promise to keep to your side of the bed, we can try sharing. It looks to be plenty big for both of us. Do you move around much in your sleep?" I walked over and sat on the bed and wondered if I made the right call. Would he keep his hands to himself? I knew I wouldn't be grabbing him in the middle of the night.

Before he could answer, alarms went off. They sounded similar to the klaxon bells on the ship but not as loud. I jumped up "What is that?"

"Battle call, we are under attack. Stay here. I must go help defend the outpost. Please don't leave the room. I would hate for you to get caught up in any of the fighting." He kissed me on the top of my head and ran out. He didn't even close the door behind him, he was in such a hurry.

I ran to the window, after closing the door, and looked out to see if I could find out what was going on. There really wasn't anything to see. If we were under attack, it must be a small group attacking one gate or something. I couldn't even hear weapons firing.

Someone knocked on my door. When I went to answer it, I found Paris loaded with weapons. "Come on. We're going to go and help defend this place."

"Who are we defending it from? It doesn't look like there is anything attacking us." I grabbed the door and shut it behind me as she pulled me with her.

"Here, take this phaser gun and a Taser too. The Taser is a one-time use thing, and it works great if a bug is on you. Much better than shooting their head off once they are on top of you." She made a screwy face, and I remembered hearing about her experience with a bug getting its head blown off while crawling on her body. Eww. I could totally empathize.

That must mean that another group of mutant cockroaches were attacking. This was not going to be a fun night. We were supposed to go to a BBQ and have ice cream, for pete's sake! Not fight the Zateelians again.

When we made our way outside, it was pandemonium. They were obviously not accustomed to battle. Aliens were yelling all over the place to try and calm the people down. Most of them looked scared to death. Kids were even running around crying and calling for their moms.

This was awful. I looked toward the closest wall, and it did seem to be manned. I could see orange bolts of energy as the warriors discharged their weapons.

Shoot, I should be inside, not out here in the middle of the battle. Zelan told me to stay in our room. I couldn't understand what Paris thought we were going to be able to help with. I had never used a gun, nor had any training. Zelan promised to show me how to use a phaser gun after we were attacked the other day, but there hasn't been time. I only knew something about the Taser because he had given me one to use. However, I never used it.

"Paris, what in the universe can I do to help? I have never even held a gun," I complained as we ran towards a wall.

"Natalie, you don't need experience. I didn't have any before last week. Now I know how to use these weapons and can kill cockroaches with no problem. Just think of it as a giant bug swatter, and it won't be a problem to kill them." She smiled at me over her shoulder, eyes sparkling and a huge grin on her face. She looked like she was enjoying this.

I followed her and started panting, "I don't have a problem killing bugs. I just don't know how to use these guns." I put one into the air and waved it about like I was holding a foam finger at a football game. My arm hurt from holding it up, so I brought it down quickly. Those phaser guns were heavier than they looked.

We made it to the wall, and I could barely hear the screeching from the other side. Those bugs weren't very loud. Our guys were yelling orders left and right and shooting into the area outside of the wall like crazy.

"Come on! We have to find a way to that walkway. They need more people who can shoot at the bugs. Most of the humans here are too used to the simple life, and they have forgotten how to handle an issue. Which really surprises me since they practically had to fight for their freedom."

"Maybe they're just tired of fighting? Or they know something about these bugs that we don't? Paris, did the Commander ever tell you how the cockroaches reproduce?" She was walking quickly to the nearest stairwell. Their stairs were made of the same shiny metal but didn't seem to make any noise as we ascended them.

"Yes, Venay told me. Did Zelan tell you?" She looked back over her shoulder at me and scowled.

"Yes, after we found those women in the jungle. The warriors had to kill them and burn their bodies in order to make sure none of the hatchlings survived. It was pretty gruesome. If I am ever infected, I hope you kill me right away and burn my body too! I don't want to give them a way to increase their numbers using my body." I shivered when the image of the women came to mind. I doubted I would ever forget the gore and horror of how a Zateelian used up a human body.

"Same here, sister! Now come on! Let's find a spot where we can kill all the insectoids in our path! But remember, you have to shoot them in the head, it's the only way to kill them." I swear that chick had blood lust or something. Her eyes were alight with excitement as she smiled. She actually smiled as she shot at the first bug she found! Then she said, "Oh, yes! Take that, sucker!"

I shook my head at her and pointed my gun and tried firing. I missed the first couple of times. Once I hit one in the head, and it exploded, I was pretty proud of myself. There was no way I would be called a great shot, but I did hit quite a few of those things. Most of them were crawling along the ground so it was difficult to aim only for their head. A lot of my shots hit the ground in front of them instead of their head.

Paris yelled at me to stop, "Natalie, look out there. There

must be hundreds still coming at us. What happened?" I looked out at the crowd and noticed how small they were.

"Paris, are those full-grown bugs? Or are they still maturing? Something tells me we won't find any more escaped people alive." I got shivers thinking about how they must have died. The thought of going through that pain and horror almost made me gag. Thank goodness we hadn't eaten dinner yet!

"You're right. They're all young cockroaches. That could work to our advantage. Venay told me that once they fully mature their carapaces are almost impossible to penetrate. However, when they're young, their bodies are still sensitive to our phasers. We don't have to only aim for their faces. Let's give it a try and see if slicing them open will kill them just as easily." She took aim at a close bug and hit its back. It stopped and was writhing on the ground.

She hit it again and it stopped moving. That gave me hope that I could actually do something more than hit dirt. I changed my aim and I ended up tearing up quite a few of those mutant things.

Somehow, Zelan found me, and he was furious. His eyes were narrowed, and his mouth was pursed. He had his hands at his side and they were clenched. "What are you doing out here? It is too dangerous for you. I told you to stay in our room." He looked at Paris and gave her the evil eye.

"Did she talk you into coming out here?" He pointed to Paris with his thumb. "She has been known to get herself into a lot of trouble. You shouldn't have followed her." He shook his head at me when I shrugged my shoulders and brought my hands up in front of me.

"She kinda dragged me along. But now that I'm here, I think I'm doing pretty good. You should see how many I've killed. Stay here with us and watch." I pointed my gun back out over the wall and started shooting them and hitting them on their backs.

"You won't kill them that way. It only slows them down," he said.

"Nuh uh, watch." I hit one I had already hit in the back a second time, and it died. "We discovered that these are all youths. Can't you tell how small they are?"

He hit his forehead and realization set in. "Of course! We have never seen them when they are young. They only send their fully mature cockroaches out to fight. Oh, crap! This means, oh no. I am so sorry."

"Yea, we figured it out already. There won't be any more humans to find out there. At least we know what happened." I shook my head and took aim again at another group headed toward us.

Zelan pushed the spot under his ear to turn on his communication device. "Commander, these are young Zateelians. It takes two shots to their body, and they die. I am going to pass the word around along the wall. Maybe you can get the warriors in the turret guns to start firing? Those should kill them easily." I heard Zelan say when he called the Commander. "Yes, sir. Thank you."

"Commander Venay also figured it out. The word is spreading. We should have these suckers exterminated shortly. The transport ship has some weapons on it, so Haver and Aysiaer are going to take it up and start firing at the largest grouping of bugs." We heard the ship coming towards us just as Zelan finished telling me about it.

I looked up and saw the turrets from their weapons take aim at a cluster and fire. Bugs and guts went flying all over the place. The warriors on the wall started cheering as we watched bug after bug die.

The three of us pointed our guns and started to take out the single cockroaches that got past the large phaser and cannon bursts. They just kept coming. How they had reproduced so many in such a short time was beyond me. I would have to remember to ask Zelan about this later.

Out of the corner of my eye, I saw one small bug trying to climb up the wall. It kept slipping. No wonder they used that metal for the wall. I had wondered about it. When we first arrived, it was a bit shiny, and I had to cover my eyes to keep them from hurting. It seemed like it would have been more of a pain than needed. Now it made perfect sense watching that cockroach slipping down the wall.

I decided to end his difficult climb. It was a perfect hit to its head, and the roach went splat. It also caught another one on its way down. I hoped none were getting inside. Paris pointed a few more out to me that had made it onto the wall.

"Natalie, let's spread out so we can target different spots along the wall as they try to climb. Zelan, make sure your guys along the wall get back to fighting. They need to get their heads out of the clouds, literally." Paris pointed to a few warriors who were watching the transport ship annihilate the bugs that were further out from the wall. I could understand why they were doing that, but they were supposed to be warriors, not spectators.

I moved down the wall a little bit, and Zelan followed me. "Natalie, I understand you want to help. However, this isn't the best place for someone who has never had to fight a day in their life." His comment actually hurt. I started to doubt myself and missed the next few shots.

"Zelan, if you can't be helpful then you can just leave. I was doing fine without you. Now, I can't concentrate." I shot again and hit one right in the eye. That was just plain gross.

Now that I was upset, I pictured Zelan's face on all of the bugs and hit them right on. Hmm, that might be the trick then. I wondered if it worked for Ben's face too. "Hot dog! It does!" I said to no one in particular.

"What's that?" Zelan asked. He moved a bit closer and noticed how many I just obliterated. "Oh, you do have skills, don't you? Sorry, I shouldn't have doubted you." He looked at me and winked.

I pictured the next one with Zelan's stupid face and blew it to bits. "Take that you stupid alien!"

"That's the way, keep killing 'em!" Zelan patted me on the back and kept shooting. How infuriating he was! The rest of the bugs I killed had his face on them. He was so condescending! Paris never treated me like that. She had faith that I could do this. I wondered if that was why Zelan wanted me to stay inside because he had no faith in me?

I scooted away from him and closer to another warrior along the wall. We needed to spread out anyway. Plus, I didn't want him watching me. If I let slip his name while I was imagining his face on those bugs, it could get awkward. He didn't need to know I was killing him over and over in my mind.

There was no time to dwell on him. One of the bugs did get over the side of the wall and attacked a warrior. I was the closest person, so I ran to him and shot at the back of the bug. It was already on top of the warrior, and what I saw next was going to stay with me a very long time. There was a tube going from the bug down the inside of the warrior's mouth. I could see something being pushed inside his body. It must have been egg sacks. I screamed as I shot its head off and the egg sack exploded all over the warrior.

He knew exactly what happened to him. His eyes were wide with shock and his mouth was still full of the reproductive organ that had been forced down his throat. He looked at me pleadingly since he couldn't talk, and his arms reached out to my gun. I knew what he wanted. There was no way I could do it. Tears built up in my eyes as I looked at him and knew exactly what was going to happen, but I wasn't strong enough to help him.

Zelan ran up behind me and saw the warrior laying there. He didn't even hesitate. His gun aimed at the guy's head, and he shot it. No warning, no apology, nothing. He shot the warrior's head multiple times to ensure that nothing survived.

Tears streaked down my face as I kept seeing the image over and over in my head. I couldn't believe how cold-hearted Zelan was. He didn't even say anything to me. I saw him take something out of his pocket and he walked over to the body and set it on fire. Then he walked back to me, took my hand, and led me away from the fire.

Once we stopped, I yanked my hand out of his, "How could you be so callous and kill him like that? You didn't even say you were sorry or ask him if he had any last words." I started crying, and he took me in his arms and held me.

"Natalie, I can't tell you how sorry I am you had to see that. Navoy was a brave warrior. It was exactly what he wanted." He sighed. "Was that the first time you have seen a person die?" He held me tight while I cried. I just nodded my head into his chest. Other than the 2 bodies we had found the other day, I had never seen a dead body, let alone watch as someone killed a person. Or alien.

He sighed, "I really wish I could help console you right now. There is nothing more I want than to take you back to our room and protect you, but I can't. I have to get back to fighting. If you want to sit next to me you can. No one will think any less of you." He kissed the top of my head and let go of me.

"No, I need to help in any way I can. If I sit here, I'll just keep crying and that won't help the settlement at all." I wiped my tears and sucked in a deep breath. "I can cry later."

I walked away from him and faced out to the battle below us and got right back to shooting the enemy. I no longer pictured Zelan's head. Now, all I saw were the disgusting bugs and my need for them to be dead. I was going to avenge that warrior's death.

CHAPTER TEN

We fought nonstop until Commander Venay came over to tell us we got the last bug. I wiped the sweat from my brow and noted at least an hour had passed since that brave warrior died. There were so many cockroach bodies out there. I wouldn't have been surprised if I'd been hitting dead bodies for the past ten minutes. I hadn't noticed any movement for a while, but I was not taking any chances after what happened to the warrior who was next to me. "Commander, there were so many of them. Is that normal?" I just couldn't understand how they reproduced so quickly.

"Sadly, yes, it is. My guess is that all of the surviving insectoids from the crashed ship impregnated every human they found. Some humans probably had multiple egg sacks put inside of them. The young grow rather quickly." He ran a hand through his hair.

"I doubt the humans got very far and were captured within hours of their escape. This is why it is so important for us to keep everyone together inside of the ship. No one wants to see this happen again." He paused as he looked out to the battlefield and shook his head.

"Not just because they attacked our settlement, but

because of what happens to the host body. We will need to send out parties to find the bodies and ensure that they are all incinerated. It is doubtful that we will find any more viable egg sacks inside the bodies, but you can never be too sure." He looked past us towards Navoy's body that was still burning.

The Commander sighed and looked over the wall. "Zelan, please take your mate back to your room." He looked back at Paris, "Paris, will you please listen to me and go with your friends? We have clean-up to do. This is not going to be pleasant. All the bodies must be burned. There is no way to tell if there are any viable egg sacks inside of those we killed. While rare, I have heard that even if you kill the body, their eggs can still hatch inside of them. We don't need any more Zateelian population explosions." He motioned for her to join him.

Paris walked up to the Commander and wrapped her arms around him. "Yes, I'll go back to the room and wait for you. Unless Natalie needs me, then I'll be in her room." She reached up and gave him a quick kiss. "I love you Venay. Please don't take too long."

He caressed her cheek with his giant hand and leaned into her. "I love you Paris with everything I am. If I could, I would go back with you. But they need help. Navoy isn't the only one we lost today. This is really bad. I think we will need to stay here for a few days to help them get back on their feet. They lost at least fifty warriors today."

I couldn't listen anymore. I turned into Zelan and started to cry.

"Shh, I am here for you, Natalie. Let's go back to our room." Zelan rubbed my back and I only grabbed him tighter before he released me.

We started to walk slowly to the stairs. Once we got to the bottom, we waited until Paris showed up. Zelan held my hand and I let him the entire way back to our room.

"I'm sorry I brought you out here, Natalie. I never should have done that. Truly, I thought it might be 100 of them, and we could quickly kill them. It should have been an easy way for you to practice shooting and get comfortable with a phaser gun. Had I known what we were up against, I probably would have stayed back with you instead of coming out here." Paris shook her head and sighed.

Speaking was not something I could do just then. I kept crying and leaned into Zelan as he walked us back to our rooms. Paris asked if I wanted her to join us, but I was not in the mood for company.

We made our way into the room, and Zelan sat me on the bed but never let go of me. I couldn't understand why I was so upset. I didn't even know the guy's name until after he was gone.

I felt like the rug was being pulled out from under me. Watching someone die in a truly vile way made me think about what was really important to me. What I thought I knew about my life was all wrong. Ben had been an absolute jerk to me. Why was I even thinking about Ben anymore? Zelan wasn't perfect, but he did have my best interests at heart. Unlike Ben.

I didn't want to be *that* girl. You know, the one who escapes into her past to avoid her present. This new me was a much stronger girl than the one I left behind on Earth. Dealing with the attack and all the death is exactly what I needed to do.

Why couldn't I get Navoy's death and burning out of my head? "Zelan, why did you burn that warrior without so much as a word?" I pushed away from him and sat up straight, and then I wiped the tears from my face. Ugh, I must have looked awful. Not that I wanted to look good for Zelan, but I could tell I had snot nose going on and my eyes must have been all swollen from the crying.

"Because that is what I would want. He was already

suffering. Having that tube down his throat and knowing what was to come. That is too difficult. He was a warrior. Showing him compassion was exactly what I did. It was exactly what I would want anyone else to do for me. If it had been me, there was nothing anyone could have said or done to ease my pain." He took ahold of my hand and gently said, "Put yourself in his shoes. What would you have wanted at that moment in time?"

I sat there for a minute thinking about it. My forehead scrunched up as I considered Zelan's words. "You're right, nothing would have mattered. If my mom was there, I would have liked to have heard her tell me she loved me one last time. But nothing else would be appropriate. I think I understand now. That must have been a tough thing to do." I turned to look at him. "Have you had to do that before?"

I could only imagine the turbulent thoughts going through Navoy's head once the bug had been killed. He knew exactly what was to come if he didn't die right away. He had probably seen too many others go through the torture of being torn apart from the egg sacks hatching. Having him wait even one more second would have been the wrong thing to do. The guy couldn't talk so why prolong his torture?

"Yes. There have been a couple of times I had to do that. Thankfully, none of the warriors had been close friends. I think that would be much harder. Even though I barely knew Navoy, it was still tough. Killing anyone is tough, especially when they are on your team. I just told myself he was already dead, and what I did was the merciful thing to do." He squeezed my hand and I gave him a hug. Until this moment, I hadn't thought about what it must have been like for him. Then I thought about Paris.

"We should invite Paris over until the commander gets back. She shouldn't be alone right now." I felt like such an idiot for being so selfish. Zelan went to her room and brought her back.

"How are you doing, Paris?" I walked up to her and gave her a hug. She hugged me back pretty hard. "I'm sorry I didn't invite you in earlier. I was so self-absorbed I didn't think about what you were going through."

She let me go and stepped back. "Don't worry about it. I had time to cry. I hate crying in front of people. So it worked out." She shrugged her shoulders. "How about you? Are you okay?"

I gave her a small smile. "Yes, I'm better now. I have never seen a dead body before this week and to watch as that bug did what it did." I shivered as I remembered it. "Well, let's just say I hope to never see a cockroach of any size again."

"How about we play some games?" Zelan asked.

"What kind of games do you have?" I didn't know anything about alien games, so I wondered what we could play.

"Some of the humans here requested Earth games a while back. So on one of our trips to Earth, we picked up a bunch of them and dropped them off here. This colony has always been the one to request the most from Earth. Others didn't seem to care as much." Zelan left Paris and me alone for only a few minutes before he came back with an armload of games.

We spent the next few hours playing various board games from Earth. I was just about to beat them in Monopoly when Commander Venay showed up. I had half of the properties with hotels on them. Both Paris and Zelan had to mortgage most of their properties in order to keep playing. They were not going to make it more than three rounds before they lost to me. Stupid commander. What rotten timing.

Paris jumped up and opened the door for him, and she threw herself into his arms. I had never seen her show so much affection for him. She must have really fallen in love with him. Or did that mate bond thing control a human's emotions?

"I'm so happy to see you Venay!" And then she kissed him, right in front of us. It wasn't just a peck on his lips either.

The Commander laughed and looked over at us, "She was losing, wasn't she?"

Zelan laughed and said, "Yes, we both were losing to Natalie."

Paris slapped the commander on his shoulder. "Couldn't I just be happy to see you? It has been a rough day."

"I am sorry, sweetheart. Of course, that is why you jumped into my arms and kissed me in front of your friends. Forgive me for assuming it was something else." He smiled and kissed her quickly on the cheek. They said their good-byes and left us alone.

"Is there any food around here? I'm finally starting to get hungry. And by food, I don't mean chalky, jello mold or food bars. I was really looking forward to the BBQ. There must be something else to eat this late at night, right?" My stomach started to grumble, loudly. "Oh, how embarrassing," I said as I grabbed my stomach.

"Let's go see what we can find. I doubt the ice cream shop or the sandwich place will be open tonight, but the canteen probably has something we can eat." He reached out for my hand, and I let him hold it. It was surprisingly comforting. Today of all days, comfort was what I needed and wanted.

It took us about fifteen minutes of wandering outside to find someplace open. The restaurant was more like a military chow hall I had seen on TV than anything else. It was a very sterile room, with lines of food along some counters. There wasn't a cash register. All food here was free.

They had grilled chicken, or what looked like grilled chicken. I requested the meat to be chopped and put on a salad, then grabbed some tea. Zelan found us a quiet table in the corner. Their hot tea tasted like chamomile and reminded me of simpler days. When I was young, my grandma used to make this for me whenever I slept over at her house. She died many years ago, but I always thought of her when I tasted chamomile.

We ate quickly and quietly. No one in the room was talking. Everyone had bleak expressions on their face. I couldn't imagine what it was like to live in this small of a community and lose so many people in one night. I bet they all knew each other too.

After dinner, we went right back to our room. Normally, I would have liked to take an evening stroll after dinner, but the mood was all wrong. Everywhere I looked people were sad or crying. I felt awful for this community, but I wasn't a part of it, so I didn't feel like I could mourn with them.

"Natalie, would you mind if I went to sleep now? I am exhausted and really need to get some sleep." Zelan rubbed my shoulders and I could tell he was tired by the lines around his eyes and the sallow look to his face.

"You know what? I was going to say the same thing. It has been a very emotional day." I took my borrowed pajamas to the bathroom to get ready for bed and thought about how awkward this sleeping situation was. He had told me earlier that he would be a gentleman. He even offered to sleep on the couch. I knew he wouldn't fit so I vetoed that idea. I chewed on my lower lip as I procrastinated leaving the room. I just hoped I wouldn't have nightmares tonight.

When I woke up, I was curled up against Zelan's side. He had an arm around me. "Good morning, sleepy head. I was wondering when you would wake up." He smiled down at me.

"Sorry, I didn't realize I had curled up against you. You could have woken me if we needed to be up sooner." I stretched and yawned.

"No worries. I was quite content with you in my arms. You are a perfect fit." He gave me a quick hug. "We don't need to be anywhere for at least two more hours. I wanted to take you to this little place that makes the best breakfast I have ever had. Have you ever eaten chocolate chip pancakes?"

I bolted upright in bed. "Are you serious? They have chocolate chip pancakes *here*?"

That was my favorite lazy day breakfast growing up. Mom would make them for the entire family on Saturdays when we had no plans. It didn't happen often, but those were the days I missed the most. We would all eat the pancakes in our pajamas, and then head off to the living room to lay around and watch movies as a family. I think my sister and I actually got along back then too.

He chuckled, "I take it you like them?"

How could he look so good first thing in the morning? His teeth were dazzling white, his hair was a perfect mess, and he didn't have sleepy eyes like I always did. I bet my hair looked like a hornet's nest right about then too. What was I thinking? It was better if I looked a mess. I didn't need him falling for me any harder than he already had.

"Yes, can I shower first?" I got out of bed so fast, it was as if a fire had been lit under my butt. Finally, I found something that reminded me of home. It was something little, but sometimes it's the small stuff that mattered the most.

For the first time in the history of the universe, a woman was ready before the man! It felt good to hurry him along. "Come on Zelan, we have to get there before they run out, or we won't have time to sit and enjoy the pancakes! Do they have real maple syrup?" I knew it was silly. Nevertheless, this was the only thing enjoyable about this trip so far.

"Calm down." He chuckled. "They have never run out before. I usually stop here for their breakfast whenever we are in town. I am not sure if it tastes the same as what you are used to. I do know that our butter and milk are different because we don't have cows. At least not like yours. Ours are called, laulons, and produce a much richer milk. Most humans won't drink ours because it is so rich. Only our young children drink the milk of laulons. It is full of vitamins a growing child needs."

"Strange, I just assumed you had the same cows as us. Well, I knew it would be a different name but thought it was the same. I'm really interested in trying this now." When our breakfast came, I wasn't let down in the least.

While it was richer and creamier than I was used to, the chocolate chip pancakes were absolutely delicious! I knew I could live here, as long as they got rid of all the Zateelians.

"Sooo, what are we doing today? No more fighting, I

hope?" I could handle it again, just not this soon. Fighting was not in my DNA.

"We are going to a memorial service for those who died yesterday, and then we will head back to our ship. I must warn you, the Commander has said that unless you agree to be my mate, you will have to go back into the cells." Zelan scratched his head, and I could tell he was sad by the downturn on his lips.

"I understand. While I'm not happy about it, I knew I wasn't going to get to stay free. Look, I do have feelings for you." He started to smile, and I put my hand up to stop him from getting too happy, "I'm not ready for a new relationship. My old fiancé, Ben, was like a cancer. I'm not saying you are anything like him. I'm sure you are the total opposite." I was wiggling in my seat.

"However, I need some time to be single and figure things out for myself. My entire adult life was with Ben. I have no clue who I am without a man. Before I can be with anyone, I need to figure myself out first. Can you understand that?" This was a truly uncomfortable situation, but he deserved the truth.

He cleared his throat. "Yes, I can understand. I am not happy, but I will respect your wishes. Does this mean you do not want to spend any more time with me?"

Oh, those sad puppy dog eyes! If I hadn't learned how strong I could be, I would have changed my mind right then and there. Zelan was a very handsome man. When his veins pulsed purple, I almost felt like I could love him. And when he pulsed blue, like right now, I felt his sadness in my heart.

There was this need inside of me to make him happy. I wasn't sure if it was a trained desire from my last relationship, or if this was because of how I felt for Zelan. These were the types of things I needed time to learn.

"No, of course not. I want to spend time with you, getting to know you. Maybe if we lived here in this settlement we could date? Could we do that on the ship? Would the Commander allow it?" I couldn't believe I hadn't thought of this before.

"Date? What is that?" I watched Zelan's veins as they pulsed back and forth between blues and greens. It really was mesmerizing. He was so cute when he tilted his head to one side and scrunched his forehead.

"Dating is a social event where a man and a woman who are interested in each other spend time together. They go out and do romantic things like candlelight dinners, mini-golf, sailing on a lake, or even making pottery together. I'm not the best at these things since my ex never did any of it. We went out in groups to parties a lot. Or out to dinner, but nothing romantic. I want to experience romance. Can you understand that?" I put my hand out to touch his hand and he lightly clasped it in between both of his.

"Yes, I understand what you are looking for. This isn't something my species is accustomed to, but I have noticed other humans, with their mates, back home doing some of what you have said. I will speak with the Commander and see what I can do." He lifted my hand and kissed the palm. It sent goosebumps down my entire body. I couldn't help but shiver and smile. Little did he know, but he did have the romance thing down.

We walked out of there holding hands like a real couple on Earth would do. I wasn't sure if that was the best thing, but I did say I wanted to date him. How was I going to do this from a jail cell?

Later that day after the tearful memorial service, we boarded the transport ship and made our way back to the *jail* ship. I missed the colony from the moment we took off. There had to be a way I could get into the colony as a worker.

We were making our landing when inspiration struck. "Paris, could I have dinner with you tonight? I have some questions about my status and how it will all work here on this planet. Is that possible? Can you come get me from jail whenever you have a chance?"

"I can get you tonight, I think. In the future, I will have to run it past Venay. He's running the entire ship, and I need to be careful about the liberties I take, even if I am his mate." Then she whispered, "Aren't you interested in Zelan?"

I leaned in closer and replied, "Yes, I am. Although, I have never been a single adult. I don't even know who I am without Ben. I want to figure this out before I accept anyone's offer of marriage."

"Then why don't you just accept Zelan's offer and sleep on his couch. That was what I did in the beginning." She had mentioned that before the crash she was sleeping on the Commander's couch, but I didn't think much about it.

While it did sound good, I wasn't sure how long I needed to be single. Or if I would eventually accept Zelan. It wouldn't be right to give him the expectation that we would marry and then for me to say I wasn't in love with him. Plus, I doubted I could go back to being a prisoner after being treated as a mate.

"Yes, but you only waited, what a week, before you married the Commander? I'm not interested in just waiting a week. Zelan and I had a great conversation over breakfast. I would love to talk to you about it and see if what I asked him is even possible. Could we do that tonight? Or tomorrow sometime?" I looked over and noticed that Zelan was smiling at me.

I returned his smile and remembered that they had excellent hearing. Everyone here probably heard what we just said. I could feel my cheeks heating up. There was no way anyone missed my blush.

Paris noticed and chuckled. "Yes. I'll get you an invite to dinner at my place tonight. Don't worry. Since we have been gone longer than expected, I doubt Venay will even be home tonight."

"Thank you, my friend." I realized that she really was my friend in every sense of the word. Hopefully, we wouldn't be separated once we got back to the V'Zenian homeworld.

Going back to the jail cell was miserable. I felt oppressed and depressed all at once. The only thing that made it tolerable was the knowledge that I would see Paris soon.

Lucy and Betty came over right away, "How was it? Did you get to meet any interesting people?" Lucy asked.

Betty asked, "How did they treat their humans? Did you get to see many of them?"

Everyone around us perked up and listened to our conversation.

"Yes, I did see how the humans live here, and if there is any way you can get a spot in that colony, you need to do it! Seriously, they are not slaves here. Every one of them works at a job and have regular freedoms like we would back home. Well, except for now. They are all required to stay inside the fences, but that's for their own safety. After the attack yesterday, I bet they are going to be looking for some more workers."

Rachelle was in the cell next to mine. She stood up and got as close as she could. "What attack? Who attacked you guys in a big colony?" She put her hands on her hips and chewed on her lower lip.

"It was the bugs. They found a way to quickly reproduce and send hundreds, if not thousands of their young cockroaches to attack the settlement. Paris and I both had to fight them off from the top of their fence. It was awful. So many got over and they killed fifty warriors and humans who lived in the settlement. They were not prepared for this attack at all." I continued to tell them about what I saw, and they were all shocked.

"But, but, how could that be? I overheard one of the

warriors talking about how the mutants reproduce. How could they have reproduced so many in such a short time?" Lucy asked.

"I don't know the specifics, but from what we saw the other day when we found those women out there in the jungle, I would say that there are no more free humans on this planet. My guess is that they were all rounded up by the Zateelians and used as breeding vessels. Zelan thought that maybe multiple bugs implanted their eggs into each person." I wasn't the only one who was grossed out. Most of those near me were shivering, and it wasn't cold in this room. A few even coughed, probably trying to hide the fact that they were gagging.

I directed the conversation back to the colony. "Our kind have normal lives and work at regular jobs. I met a woman named Clarissa who's a receptionist in a regular office building. They have human architects who are designing new buildings here and sending their designs to the V'Zenian homeworld. They have restaurants, and even regular BBQ's where everyone gets together for the evening and has fun. We were supposed to have one last night, but the cockroaches ruined it!" I pounded my fist against my thigh. Still thinking about the attack upset me.

A few of the women smiled, but most sat there thinking. Rachelle spoke up, "Do you think we will have a chance to stay here and get regular jobs? Do they have any industries there, or manufacturing?" She seemed to be very interested in this new turn of events. Her hands were holding the bars pretty tightly, and she was focused on the conversation. Even the male jail handlers, who she normally kept one eye on so she could flirt with, had lost her attention.

"I did see industry, but I couldn't tell you what they make, or if they actually manufacture anything." We all spent the next hour or so discussing the things I saw while I tried to answer their questions. Most of which I couldn't. I told them

I would be seeing Paris soon and would ask her if any of us could move to the settlement.

Zelan came to get me. He smiled at me and opened the door to my cell. "Natalie, come on. We are both invited to dinner with the Commander and his mate."

I raised one eyebrow. "Oh really? The Commander will be there?" I asked as I walked out, not sure if I liked that idea. He usually intimidated me. "I thought he was going to be really busy tonight since we were gone so long? At least, that's what Paris thought."

"He had planned to work late until he heard your conversation with Paris. I think he might like the idea of sending all of you humans to the settlement when half of our warriors go later this week."

I stopped and put a hand on his arm. "Wait, half of you guys are going to the settlement? Why?"

"They need our help. Until we have eradicated those bugs, the civilians are in real danger, especially the children. Commander Venay wants to set up a training regimen for all the settlers. That way they can learn to defend themselves. Even once we eradicate the bugs, they still have other animals on this planet which are quite deadly." He continued to walk, and I followed him.

"That makes sense. If we can be given the same freedoms as all of the other people living there, then I know that everyone will want to go and get jobs. I'm sure some will even be happy to marry or mate with V'Zenians. Especially if they learn how to woo a lady." I raised my eyebrows suggestively at him.

His veins pulsed purple as his smile grew, and he reached for my hand. We walked hand in hand the rest of the way there.

Paris answered the door. "Natalie, I'm so happy you could make it tonight." She smiled and acted like this was some regular dinner party where I was invited but didn't RSVP for. Strange.

"Um, I just saw…" She put up her hand to quiet me and invited me in. I almost stopped dead in my tracks. There was Captain Montgomery, the former leader of this ship. He was worse than Commander Venay. I got the impression he didn't like humans.

Zelan did his strange military salute, where he put his right fist over his heart, and then bowed slightly. "Commander, Captain, it is an honor to be invited to your dinner tonight."

I stayed quiet since I didn't know the protocol for this. The Commander came over and put his hand out for me to shake. "Commander, thank you for the dinner invitation." I almost curtsied but remembered he was military, not royalty.

The Captain came over and shook my hand too. "Nice to formally meet you, Captain. What an honor it is for me to have dinner with such prestigious company." Thankfully, my mother taught me how to kiss up when in the presence of powerful men.

Paris took my hand and brought me into the kitchen with her while the men stayed in the living room chatting in their native tongue. I still needed to get my universal translator installed. Maybe I could get that tomorrow or the next day. One more way to keep out of the prison cells.

"Paris, what's going on?" I looked back at the men, and over to Paris who had plastered a smile on her face.

"I think that a large group of us are going to be asked to volunteer to head over to the settlement for the next few months. You might want to consider it." She kept her voice low, so as not to attract the attention of the men in the other room.

"Are you going? Or staying?" I was very tempted to go, even if Paris didn't.

"Honestly, I don't know. I think Venay and the Captain are discussing that tonight. Either way, Zelan is going to be heading up the mission. Although, I'm not sure he knows that yet. So, keep it quiet until they ask him. It's a really great opportunity for him. Here, he is highly ranked but not in charge of the warriors. On Venay's ship, he was in charge of the warriors. He created their schedule and conducted the daily training. I think he misses it." She was preparing some sort of meal in the replicator. It looked like it might be a pot roast.

"Did they get the replicators from our old ship while we were gone?" I wondered.

"Yes, one was installed here, and two were installed in the mess hall. All of our friends will get human food starting tomorrow." She smiled from ear to ear. Her excitement was evident in the way she kept moving around and smiling.

"That is great news." My stomach responded its appreciation as well with a nice rumble. "Well, I guess that was an approval of the smell at least. It does smell great."

"I'm glad you approve. Help me carry the dishes out to the table?" Paris asked.

"Sure."

Dinner went rather smoothly, and Zelan even brought up the subject of my universal translator. "Natalie, now that we are back, have you thought about getting a universal translator installed?" I noticed the Captain was paying particular attention to me.

"Yes, I was actually just thinking about that. Is there a way to do it tomorrow or the next day?" I hadn't heard of any issues from Paris, so I figured it was probably safe. More women had been getting them implanted since we arrived on this ship. I was a bit leery at first, but now I thought it might be smart.

"Natalie, how did you like your time at the New Hope settlement? Did you find it relaxing? Or enjoyable? I understand you pretended to be mated to Zelan in order to stay with him," the Captain asked.

My cheeks heated up very quickly. "Yes, it was an interesting time. Dealing with the attack on the settlement changed the entire stay. Paris and I both took up positions on the wall and helped to kill quite a few mutant cockroaches."

"Really, I hadn't heard you both fought. I assumed that you would have stayed back in the safety of your rooms." He turned his head toward the Commander, "You allowed your mate to fight? But she isn't trained. Please tell me she didn't get in the way of your leading the defense of the city." I saw what he was up to, he wanted to get the Commander out of the picture and was trying to make him out to be a bad leader.

"Actually, Paris is quite adept at defending herself as well as anyone else in her care. She was on a different part of the wall with Zelan and Natalie. From what I understand, they killed quite a few Zateelians. In fact, Paris and Natalie both figured out we were battling young bugs right about the time that I did. I had just given the intel to Captain Mypo to disseminate when Zelan called to tell me. Zelan was able to relay the news to his side of the wall quite easily, and they worked together to kill more than their fair share. I will always be happy to have her watch my back in battle." Venay puffed his chest out, but I could tell he was eyeing the Captain suspiciously.

"Thank you, Venay. I hope I can live up to your kind praise." She bowed her head toward him. I hadn't seen her act so compliant before. There must be more going on here than I understood. I knew the Captain was a jerk, but why care about impressing him?

"Interesting. Well, maybe we should send more slaves to the settlement and have them help guard the families. I wonder if they would really help or use the opportunity to kill our species." What was he thinking? Why in the world would we kill their families! I swear, if I ever got the chance, I was going to kick that man in his family jewels. He seriously needs to be taken down a peg or two.

I looked over to Paris and rolled my eyes. She just smiled.

The Commander stood up and picked up his glass of water. "I would like to propose a toast to our newest Captain." He looked over to Zelan who was positively beaming.

Well, I guess Paris didn't know all of the news. And why didn't Zelan tell me about his promotion when he picked me up earlier?

We all picked up our glasses and cheered to his new promotion. Both the Commander and Zelan were pulsing green, but the Captain was going back and forth between orange and dark blue. I knew that orange meant he was frustrated. The dark blue must have meant he was despondent. Strange that he would be upset over Zelan's promotion.

As soon as we were done with dinner, the Captain said his goodbyes, and everyone in the room breathed a sigh of relief once the door closed.

"Venay, I don't trust that man. He gives me the creeps the way he looks at us women. I get the feeling he just wants slaves, not mates or helpers. Please never leave me on this ship alone with him." Paris walked over to the Commander and put her arms around his torso.

He put his around her and leaned down to kiss the top of her head. "He isn't a fan of humans. I promise I will never leave you with that man. Like I said back on our ship, you are not to leave my side until we get off this planet." They really did make a cute couple.

Paris looked to me. "Natalie, you said you had some things you wanted to discuss with me? Why don't we go into the kitchen and talk?" She nodded her head into the kitchen, and I followed her.

"What was up with the Captain at dinner? If he hates us

so much, then why did he join us?" I had brought some plates with me and put them in the alien dishwasher contraption.

"I think he felt like he had to come. Venay didn't order him, but when your commander invites you to dinner, you don't say no." She shrugged her shoulders.

"I guess. Why did the Commander invite him?"

"Venay told me that he wanted to try and bridge the gap between us all. Make him see that humans weren't so bad. Something tells me his plan didn't work." She blew her bangs out of her eyes.

"So, when did Zelan get his promotion? I never heard them discuss it until the end of dinner." I was really excited for Zelan and couldn't wait to tell him so.

"Maybe they offered it to him while you were helping me get dinner prepared? That could be why the Captain was upset too. I heard them talking before you got here, and he wanted his Lieutenant to get the job and the promotion."

I stopped working on the dishes and looked over my shoulder to make sure no one was coming in the room. "Do you think I should go to the settlement? It's what I wanted from the moment we stepped foot in their village. If the Captain is mad at Zelan, do you think he will try to take it out on me?" The only thing that gave me pause was the fact that Zelan was going and he would expect me to spend my time with him. Not that he had told me as much, but I knew enough to know he'd give me very little time to myself.

While I did want to get to know him better, this constant pushing us together was starting to rattle my nerves. No one listened to what I said. It's almost like when we stepped on this planet, we stepped back fifty years and women could no longer be on their own. They had to have a man taking care of them.

Even Paris seemed to enjoy her alien taking care of her.

"I wouldn't put it past him. In his mind, you are still just a slave. It might be better if you chose to mate with Zelan sooner rather than later." She stopped what she was doing and looked at me with pursed lips and narrowed eyes.

I sighed. "I know that's what I am supposed to do, but I wish everyone would let me take the time I need to get over Ben. It's not that I was in love with the man, but he was the only boyfriend I ever had as an adult. Can we stop bringing this up? When I'm ready, I'll let you and Zelan know." I huffed and slapped the dish towel on the counter.

"I'm sorry, Natalie. That wasn't very nice of me. I guess there are so few of us who are mated, that I was thinking about myself in this case. It was just that I wanted more nights like tonight. Well, without the Captain." She started to laugh, and I smiled.

"Okay, just let me go at my own pace, alright?"

"Of course, forgive me?" She asked.

"Always." We hugged and finished the dishes.

Paris grabbed a couple of teas, and then we both sat at her kitchen table.

"Alright, here is what I wanted to know. If I moved to the settlement, would I have free rein of the place like the other humans who live and work there?" The tea cup in my hand was warm and it felt really good to hold it.

"I think so. But you would need to talk to Venay about that one." She took a sip of her tea and put the cup down on the table.

"Zelan and I spoke today. I want to date him and get to know him." I put my hand up to stop Paris from saying anything. "Slowly. If he is going to the settlement, then I guess I should too. It was actually what I was hoping to do. That place was almost like home. Well, besides the mutant bugs who attacked the place and killed a bunch of people." I scrunched my nose and sighed. The colony really was a great place. If I was never to go home, then this was where I wanted to stay.

"Was it the chocolate chip pancakes that sold you on the place?" Paris started to giggle, and I followed suit.

"Yes, it was. But even meeting people like Clarissa made me feel like that could be home. If things don't work out with Zelan, at least I will have a place I can fit in. You know what I mean?"

"Yes, I do. It was the kind of place I would like to settle down in as well. Too bad Venay is a ship's commander. He won't be able to stay here longer than the five months. But if you stayed here, I would see you twice a year when we made our trips to Earth." Her smile faltered as she thought about it.

"I couldn't be with Zelan if he joined you guys on that ship and started abducting people. There's no way I could support that." I shook my head.

"Do you think I can support it? Because I can't. I'm just biding my time for a chance to make a difference and change the status quo." Paris sat up straight and a determined look crossed her face.

"Really, you think you can make a change?" How could she? It wasn't like she married the V'Zenian President or anything.

"Yes, I do. I may not be able to stop it right away, but I think I could have a hand in who he chooses. Maybe I can get people to volunteer. I was thinking of a way to gather volunteers without telling them it's for a *mission to Mars*, so to speak."

"Hmm, that's interesting. I bet you could find a lot of volunteers. But you can't keep it from them. Once they are on the ship, they'll figure it out, and then you would have a riot on your hands." I was sure there were quite a few people like Sheila who would jump at a chance to leave the planet and start over on some distant, alien planet, as long as they were treated well.

"Yeah, but if we don't say anything until after we have vetted them, I'm hopeful that we will get most of them to agree to go. I was thinking we could look for those who had no family and were without a job. Start there since there are so many. Shoot, we could even take a bunch off the streets. I had some friends who might want to go." Paris probably knew a lot of people who needed a better situation than living on the street.

As I thought more about her situation, I realized this was much better for her, even with all of the dangers and having to deal with slavery. She was safe, much safer than being homeless. And she had someone who truly loved her and was looking out for her.

"Tell me, do you have a plan on how you're going to do this?" I asked.

"Not exactly. I do still have almost six months before I have to know what I'm going to do. If you come up with some ideas, I'll be very happy to hear them."

As I sipped my tea I thought about the situation. "Maybe by the time you guys leave here I'll have something for you. Do you think I'll get to see much of you when I go to New Hope?"

She smiled and took another sip before answering. "Yes. I expect we will make regular trips over to see you all. I know they have their own Commander, but Venay really wants to help make sure they have the best defense possible. Since he has seen other outposts, he has some ideas to help them. Maybe you can be on our team? You know, be Venay's personal assistant when he's there and handle things for him when he's gone? That would be a great job for you!"

"I was an accountant before the abduction. Running numbers is my thing. Tax returns on Earth? Sure, I can do that. But helping to run an alien outpost? I don't think that's in my wheelhouse." I shook my head and drank my tea.

"You have a degree don't you?"

"Yes, I have a Master's. But that isn't going to help me be a personal assistant. The skill set is very different." I hadn't been out of college long, less than a year. But I was good at what I had done so far.

"I didn't mean it was something you learned in college, I just meant that you have the ability to learn. You're a very smart woman. Believe you can do this, and you can. Something tells me a personal assistant here is very different from one back home. Just because someone on Earth is a PA doesn't mean that they could do it here. Just like you couldn't do their taxes for them. It's a very different kind of job that will require learning new skills. Let's talk to Clarissa when we get there. I'm sure she can help you figure it all out." Paris was intelligent. If only she could have gone to college I bet the sky would have been the limit for her.

"Paris, why do you want me to do this job so badly?" I scrunched my eyes, as I looked at her, wondering what was up.

"Because, I trust you to be faithful to Venay. He's going to need someone to be his eyes and ears and who won't try to stab him in the back. I think this Captain might be after his job. Plus, I'll get to see you in a much better environment." Her eyes narrowed when she mentioned the Captain and I had to agree. He was up to no good.

"That Captain would be crazy to go against the Commander. He would never win. Your Commander is so much stronger and more menacing than the Captain. Plus, I think the men will follow Venay over that idiot any day." I shook my head and remembered why I always hated politics back home.

"Which is probably why the Captain is after Venay. He's jealous. When I first met him, I thought he would be a nice, proper gentleman. But he just wanted to make a good first impression. Or maybe to see if there was a way to get between me and Venay." Paris seemed to be able to read people well. A talent that would come in handy as the mate of a Commander. She was a much better political mate than I ever would be.

The realization that they were meant to be together hit hard. I hadn't thought much about their strengths and weaknesses, but they really did accent one another. Her strengths will bolster him, and his strengths would serve to help her as well. I was starting to see a perfect match and I wanted what they had … one day.

"You know, I really hoped we had left that petty stuff behind us, there's a woman in our prison section who wants to get her claws into Zelan too. I guess *human* nature isn't just for humans is it?" I shook my head and chuckled thinking about Rachelle and what she was going to do now that we might have some freedom.

Even though I wasn't ready to mate with Zelan, it didn't mean that I wanted her to keep going after him. What I needed was another alien to distract her. I wondered if I could get Aysiaer to keep her busy for a while. He was a huge flirt. They might actually make a good couple.

As I sipped my tea, Zelan came in and sat down next to me. "Natalie, have you and Paris discussed moving to New Hope?"

"Yes, I want to go with you although not as your mate. Is that alright?" I reached out and took his hand and watched as his veins pulsed purple before turning a bit red.

He squeezed my hand. "Yes, I think we can arrange that. What type of job were you thinking about trying out for?"

What did red mean? I wanted to ask him that, and I almost did. "Paris thinks I should be Commander Venay's personal assistant. What do you think?"

His smile grew wide, and his veins went back to a beautiful purple again. "I think that is a great idea. We were just talking, and we agreed to share an assistant. If you got the job, we would work together every day."

I looked over to Paris who was smiling behind her cup of tea.

"I see. That might be interesting. How would that work if you and I are dating?" I scratched the back of my head and narrowed my eyes at Paris. I bet she knew this already.

Back home, I never would have dated someone in my office, let alone a boss. HR would have put a stop to it if they ever got wind of any sort of romantic entanglement.

"It would be great. We could spend more time together and get to know each other much better." He squeezed my hand and I felt a zing from him. Not like if he had scraped his feet along the carpet and it was a static shock, but more of something that started in my stomach from a flutter.

"You don't have any rules against workplace dating?" I bit my lip not sure how I felt about this new bump.

"No, we don't normally date our mates. Once we meet our mate, we make plans for the ceremony, and within a couple of weeks, are mated and living together." He winked at me and I could feel the heat creeping up my neck.

"Do mates work together in your society?" Paris asked.

"Sometimes, I guess when the warrior goes on a long mission, like the trips to Earth, they do take their mate with them. Sometimes the female gets some sort of job on the ship. Everyone contributes in some way. But there are no issues if you happen to work with your mate." He got up, fixed himself some tea, and came back to our table.

"Would the Commander consider hiring me?" I asked.

Speaking of the devil … he walked in at that point. No doubt he had been listening to our conversation. "Yes, I would. Paris was right. I think it is important to have an assistant who is loyal to me. None of the males who served under the Captain would be as trustworthy as you. Especially since you will most likely mate with Zelan. It is a perfect situation. If you want the job, it is yours." He grabbed a tea and joined us.

"Great, is everyone trying to force me to marry Zelan?" I pulled my hand back from him and looked at my lap.

"Natalie, I understand your hesitation, however you are in a very different situation than anything you have ever experienced on Earth. If you go to my homeworld and are not mated to one of my men, you will be a slave. There are no settlements on my planet where humans are treated as equals. You would be treated as cattle, and you would not be allowed to roam freely. In fact, Paris would not be allowed to associate with you. Not because I said no, but because your master would not allow it." The commander looked at me with that forceful look of his that always sent the bad kind of shivers down my spine. I rubbed my left arm with my right hand as I thought about what he said.

"What about staying on at the settlement? Is that a possibility?" I straightened my back and looked him in the eye when I asked.

"It could be ... but highly doubtful. Once I leave, Commander Croso will take over what I started. He won't need me, and he won't need you either." Venay took a drink of his tea. The aliens didn't seem to sip, they only guzzled what they drank. The heat must not have been an issue for their mouths.

"I see. So, unless I want to be a slave, I have to mate with Zelan." I nodded my head as I blew my hair out of my eyes.

"No, it could be another warrior. You will be able to meet a good number of males at the colony. If Zelan isn't the one for you."

Zelan started to stir in his chair and the Commander gave him the "look" which caused him to sit still. "I highly suggest you figure out what you want before my new ship arrives."

I chewed on my bottom lip and wondered if it would be so bad to accept Zelan. Although, I still had five months to figure this out. I wasn't going to worry about it tonight. "Okay, I have some time, so how about I worry about tomorrow first? Will I be able to get my universal translator?"

The Commander smirked. "It's about time you agreed to it. There are some on the planet who don't speak English, so this will make your job much easier." He got up and put his hand out for Paris, who stood up and grabbed it.

"Natalie, I'll stop by tomorrow after your surgery and see how you're doing." Paris walked off with the Commander and left me alone with Zelan.

"Come on, I will take you back to your cell, then tomorrow I will come and get you for the procedure." I had a lot to think about and he was gracious enough to stay quiet for the walk back.

We walked around a corner and I wasn't paying attention since I was so focused on everything the Commander and Zelan gave me to think about tonight. I almost walked right into a crate on the ground. Zelan gently picked me up and carried me over the crate and set me down. Ben would have just let me walk into it and hurt myself. Zelan was always looking out for me, even in the small things.

I put my hand on his arm. "Thank you, Zelan. That was very gracious of you." I smiled and we continued on our way.

CHAPTER TWELVE

True to his word, first thing in the morning Zelan came to get me. The doctor was ready. He told me I was the first of ten girls who wanted the implant today, and the rest of the week was already filling up fast.

Word spread when I got back last night. I told my cell mates about the possibility of living at the settlement and having actual jobs, *not* working as slaves. Everyone was very excited and lined up, literally, to get their universal translators.

"Doc, will this hurt?" I was a bit of a baby when it came to needles, and I couldn't imagine what was going to happen. The doctor explained it to me, but I all I could think of were the needles.

"It will pinch just a little, but after that, you won't feel anything. Even when you wake up you won't be in pain, just a bit groggy." He patted my shoulder like I was a little twelve-year-old. I expected to wake up and find a lollypop waiting for me. Oh, come to think of it, that *would* be nice.

He was right. I wasn't in any pain. Groggy was a good word for what I felt. At first, everything had this miasma over it. Then I slowly opened and closed my mouth, licking my lips. I blinked a few times to try and remove the haze, but it took a good hour to go away.

"Hi, there! How are you feeling?" Paris came in way too chipper for any patient after surgery and sat in the chair next to my bed. That bed was the most comfortable thing I had been on since this all started. Well, except for that one night with Zelan. Nothing compared to sleeping in his arms.

"Paris, it's so nice of you to come visit. How long do I stay here? Can I arrange to sleep overnight in this bed? It's quite comfortable. Much better than that jail cell." I almost shivered thinking about going back there, but my body was too relaxed.

"Sorry, they'll kick you out in a couple of hours. I might be able to get you released to my care, if Venay agrees. We could start working on your new job tomorrow. I think that would be reason enough to have you staying with me." She smiled at me, which caused me to smile.

Paris really did have a nice smile. I was surprised that no one back on Earth wanted to take care of her after her parents died. She was such a sweet and helpful person. Their loss, and my gain.

"Sounds good to me. Anything to get out of that cell. When are we leaving?" If we could go in the next few days, it would mean a much better life for everyone.

Paris pointed to a flower on the table next to my bed. "Did Zelan leave that for you?"

I turned my head. "I don't know. You're the first person I've seen since the surgery. I don't know who else would do it." It was a pretty flower. Reminded me of a hibiscus.

"I bet it was him. Venay said that Zelan was on duty this afternoon until later on tonight. I bet he came by and visited you while you were still out of it." She smiled at me with that knowing smile of hers.

"Well, if he did, that was nice of him." Inwardly, I sighed. I didn't want Paris to know how much I appreciated the flower. There was no need to give Zelan any ideas of what might melt my heart.

"Alright, I'm gonna try to talk Venay into transporting all of the people who have implants already. Maybe as early as tomorrow. He has to coordinate with the settlement leaders. There are a lot of logistics that need to be figured out. Like, where will everyone sleep? Aysiaer came by today and picked up a load of warriors to take back. Those guys will get apartments. But the humans will most likely have to live in the old barracks until more apartments are constructed." Paris seemed to know a lot about what was going on. Did Venay tell her everything, or just what he thought she needed to know?

"Oh, I guess I didn't think about living arrangements. Does that mean I'll be sharing a room with a bunch of women again?" I chuckled. "At least there won't be bars, and I'll have a bed instead of the floor. That's something, right?" I held up a hand. "Wait, there won't be bars, will there?"

"Yes, it will be much better. And no to the bars. Zelan is getting a nice, big apartment since he's a Captain now. Maybe you can visit him often, even when he isn't home." She smirked at me, and I sighed. She wasn't going to give up on this subject.

"Whatever. You know pushing me isn't going to work. I'll move in with him when I am good and ready, not a moment before." I really wished everyone would stop trying to force me into marrying, or mating, with Zelan. It was just like back home. *Why can't I choose who I want to be with instead of always being told who I have to be with?*

"You two just make a cute couple. That's all." She held her hands up as I tried to give her the evil eye. "Okay, I won't push."

Sadly, my attempt to scrunch my nose and eyebrows at her felt more like a drunken expression, thanks to the meds they had me on. "Fine, let's move on. When can I get out of here? If I'm going to your place, I would like to leave soon."

"The nurse has to come by and make sure your implant is working properly and then you should be able to leave. I can go see if she's available if you like?" Paris stood up to leave.

"Yes, thanks, Paris."

It took another hour for the nurse to show up, but as soon as she was done, I was let loose. And I do mean loose! Once we made it back to her quarters the Commander told me I had free run of the ship now. I felt so good to be told I was no longer a slave.

"Paris, what should we do now? I want to run all over this place and shout from every corner that I'm free." I laughed and did a little twirl. I'll admit, that was pretty childish, but a week in those cells will change a person.

"First off, calm down. Secondly, I think we should have a movie night in the mess hall. They have a TV there that we can use to watch some of the Earth movies Venay loaded up for me. We can also make popcorn and invite a bunch of the warriors to join us. It would be a great time for you to meet some more of the guys who will be joining you at New Hope." She winked and I knew she wasn't going to stop until I was mated with someone, even if it wasn't Zelan.

I rolled my eyes and sighed. I would just have to find a way let her matchmaking schemes pass me by. I wanted some time as a single lady, I didn't want to run from one man right to the next and never have any time for fun. To be honest, I wanted to date around. Meet several aliens before choosing a partner for life. How else was I to know who was right for me?

"That sounds like a perfect night! Almost like a night out back home. I could get used to this." I felt lighter than I had since I was first abducted. It was amazing how much I took my freedoms for granted back home.

◇◇◇

Oh, this was going to be an awesome night! There were hot warriors everywhere, and they were *not* looking to put me in chains!

"Paris, where's Zelan?" I looked around for the big lug but didn't see him anywhere.

"He's still on duty. Why? Do you want him here to hold your hand?" She said in a childish sing-song voice.

"Actually, the opposite. I was hoping to be able to flirt a little without having him turn all caveman on me." I smiled at a guy I hadn't seen before, and his veins turned red. "Paris, what does a red vein mean?"

She laughed and said, "Do you really want to know? It might make a difference in how you view tonight."

I smiled and said, "Yes, it's been bugging me. I love it when Zelan turns purple, but the red gives me a strange vibe. One I'm not sure I like."

Another hot alien walked past me towards the microwave, and his veins went from green to red as he checked me out.

She gave me a devilish smile, "It means they are turned on. So be careful with the warriors who are flashing red. I would say have fun with the guys who are purple for sure! That means love or adoration. Green is friendly or comfortable. That is a good color for just a flirt. If you don't want more, be careful you don't lead anyone on. Once they learn that a certain Captain has his eye on you, they'll stop flirting." She winked at me and went to turn the TV on.

I hadn't flirted since high school. When you're told who you're going to marry at the ripe old age of seventeen, you don't get too many chances to flirt after that.

Although, there was that one spring break in college. I

went to Cozumel with a group of girlfriends, and we met a lot of hot guys on the beach. Flirting was definitely something I did that week. It was supposed to be my week for fun in the sun, and it truly was. However, this was different. I will be working with these guys going forward. How weird would it be if I flirt with them all tonight, and then two days from now, fly to the colony with them?

I've said it before and I'll say it again, it's a darn good thing that my veins didn't pulse out colors demonstrating me emotions for all to see. Two very tall and extremely good-looking alien guys walked up to me and introduced themselves. One guy was flashing red, "Hi, my name is Balin. It's nice to finally meet you, Natalie." He reached out to shake my hand.

"How did you know my name?" I was certain Paris hadn't used it since we arrived.

"Who doesn't know your name? You are to be the new assistant to our Commander, a pretty important job. Everyone is going to want to meet you tonight." He tried to put his arm around my shoulder, "Stick with me, and I will keep away the piranhas."

It was strange, my universal translator was installed only that morning, but listening to them speak in their own tongue and hearing the translation inside my head was a bit much. It was like trying to listen to two different conversations at once. The nurse did tell me it would take a while to get used to the translation. What I didn't expect was a small ache in my head while Balin spoke.

I moved away from his arm. "I would actually like to meet everyone. Especially if I am to work with them all."

The other guy was chuckling under his breath. "Hi, I am Eshen. Pay no attention to my friend. He can be a jerk at times, but he's harmless."

I raised my eyebrows at him. He was flashing green so I

felt a bit more comfortable with him, even though he was defending the other guy.

"Are you the one I need to watch out for then?" I tried to smile in a seductive way, but since I have never tried to be seductive before, I doubted it worked.

Eshen laughed. "Sorry, I think you have us confused. He is the one to watch out for, but he would never hurt you. He might try to convince you that you are his mate, but that is as far as it would go."

"I see. Well I don't want to be anyone's mate. If you will excuse me, I see Paris has the movie started." I walked away from them thinking this could be fun, if not totally over-whelming.

"Natalie, come join us." Paris waved me over. She had saved me a seat next to her and a couple other guys. "You met my bodyguard, Golen, and this is Maximillian and Zelion. They're twins!"

"Please call me Max." One twin reached up to shake my hand, and his brother eyed me up and down while pulsing a very deep red.

Zelion said in a seductive voice, "You can call me anytime."

I rolled my eyes at him.

"Um, those Earth movie pick-up lines don't really work, Zel," Paris said while she was chuckling at him.

"Paris, have you been showing them Earth movies? Or was that the Commander's influence?" I eyed them all and wondered if Zelion had ever had a chance to use that stupid line before or if was his first.

"Oh, it was Venay's alright. He even has a copy of the old "B" movie, *Earth Girls Are Easy!*" Paris rolled her eyes and chuckled.

I busted up laughing. "I can't believe you guys watched that one. You do know it was a cheesy movie even when it was made, and we are nothing like that movie, right?" I looked at both Max and Zel, who seemed a bit sheepish.

"Well, I did wonder if that was true or not. Now I know. I haven't seen anyone from Earth since I joined the fleet. This is my first tour with the Commander, before this I was on the *Zelus Free*, patrolling the border with the Zateelians. The only humans I knew growing up were actually pretty easy." He looked at his brother and hit him on the arm. "Am I right?"

I shook my head at them as they laughed. "Somehow I doubt they were easy. Let me guess, you have never even kissed a human girl?"

Paris high-fived me, and we both laughed as Zel's veins flashed orange, before they turned to a deep forest green.

"Alright, quiet down now. We have a great movie to watch tonight. I specifically chose *Independence Day*, just for you guys." She raised her eyebrows at me, and I stifled a grin, knowing exactly what she was up to.

This was going to be fun!

I loved this movie as a kid, but watching it with actual aliens who could invade my world, made it that much more intense. As we sat there watching, the aliens started to grumble that it was lame. "Oh come on! We don't have shields like that. Who do they think they are fighting?"

"Max, they aren't fighting you guys. Just wait until you see the aliens. They are more like the insectoids crossed with a species who has tentacles. We made them up, silly. Along with the technology of the invaders." I shook my head at them. Men.

"Oh, well, yeah the Q'tueliens do have similar shields." He went back to watching the movie, and I looked over to Paris.

She shrugged her shoulders, and I mouthed, "Seriously? Another species?"

Max shushed us and pointed to the screen. He was obviously engrossed now that he knew the aliens were someone else.

Once the movie was over, I asked Zel, "So, there is an alien species out there that looked similar to the ones from this movie?" I pointed to the movie screen.

"Similar, but not exactly. We have a truce with them, but some of the technology of those Zateelians was similar to the Q'tueliens ships. So it is possible our truce is over. If so, I will have to remember the weakness from the movie. Maybe it is the same." He shook his head as he continued to watch the movie credits.

"Zel, you do know that movies aren't real, right? This was not some historical re-enactment. It was just fiction." I guess I know who got the brains when that ovum split in two.

"Huh? I thought it was a documentary. That was what Paris told us. That we were going to see a movie based on an event from your planet's history." He scratched his cute head. Both of them were really cute. Sad Zel wasn't a bit brighter.

"Um, we have never had a known encounter with aliens, unless you believe in Roswell."

Max piped up, "What is Roswell?"

Paris covered her mouth and tried to hide her little laugh. "It was where a spaceship tried to land on Earth, but we shot it down about 75 years ago. The aliens we found were taken to a top-secret base and dissected."

I kept a straight face, trying to tell myself this was a true story.

Commander Venay walked in at that point, "She is right. Another species did try to land on Earth back in their year 1947. One of my ancestors was on a ship that orbited their moon watching. That was when we decided they weren't ready for us yet, and probably never would be."

"Nuh uh! That isn't true. It was just a story I was telling Zel." He believed anything about Earth that came from a movie. Zel was so gullible. "Hey, Zel, I have a bridge I'd like to sell you back on Earth. It might help you get places faster." I couldn't keep a straight face, and neither could Paris. We both broke down laughing. The guys all looked at us like we were nuts. Maybe we were.

"Venay, did you guys really witness an alien get shot down over Roswell back in the forties?" Paris narrowed her eyes at him.

"Yes, but that is a story for another day. Let's go home, I have to get up early tomorrow to prepare the next group of troops for the colony." He started to walk away with Paris but looked over his shoulder. "Golen, I expect you to take good care of my new assistant. Bring her back to my residence when she is ready to leave."

He turned around after he saw all the warriors ogling me. "You should all know that Captain Zelan has claimed her as his mate. Make sure she is treated with respect." He smiled at me and walked out.

Oh, that man, alien, whatever! He was pushing to get me to agree to mate with Zelan too! At this rate, I would have no other options even if I wanted them. Both Max and Zel moved a bit further away from me. Great, no more harmless flirting for me.

Once the Commander and Paris were gone, I looked at the warriors around me who had gone quiet. "You know, just because Zelan likes me, doesn't mean I'm going to be his mate. I haven't said yes." I crossed my arms over my chest. This wasn't fun anymore.

"Yes, but you will. It is only a matter of time. Most human women take a couple of weeks at most to succumb to the pull of the mating bond. If you are his true, fated mate then you won't be able to stay away from him." Max patted me on the shoulder and then stood up. "I am tired and have an early morning. It is time I went back to my room. Especially since Captain Zelan is probably on his way here now. If the Commander is done for the night, then the

Captain will be too." He waved at me as both he and his brother left.

I overheard the two guys from earlier. They were talking in their native tongue. However, my universal translator worked just fine. "Balin, don't. She isn't worth the trouble you will get into if Zelan finds out you messed with his mate."

"She is beautiful and sitting all alone. What can it hurt if I just go keep her company? It's not like I plan to bring her back to our room for the night or anything. I just want to have some fun. Lighten up Eshen. It's just a little harmless flirting." Out of the corner of my eye, I could have sworn he winked at his friend before getting up.

I wanted to have fun but I wasn't sure if he was my speed or not. He sat down next to me. "Hey there. I don't blame you for not wanting to mate with Zelan. He can be a dud. I don't think I have ever seen him relax and have fun." He moved his arm behind me. Which reminded me of some lame 80's movie. I almost laughed. Instead, I moved back just a little bit.

"Zelan is actually a nice guy, and we did have fun when we were in New Hope the other day." I did enjoy my time with Zelan.

"That's cool. It's nice to hear that he can loosen up a bit. But what do you say to having some fun with me before you leave? I am staying here so I won't get to see you again for a while." He moved closer to me again, and I was about to get up when Golen interrupted.

"Excuse me, Balin, but I think it is time I took Natalie back to the Commander's quarters. I think they will all be up quite early tomorrow." Golen pursed his lips and put his hands on his hips.

"Yeah, yeah, I know." Balin waved him off before standing up. He put his hand out to help me get up and I accepted.

However, he did not let go of my hand once I was up.

Instead, he cupped it in-between both of his. "Natalie, if you want to spend time with another male let me know. I think you and I could have a lot of fun before you leave. And I won't claim you as my mate… well unless you want me to." He winked, and then leaned in to kiss my cheek.

I felt eyes on the back of my head. It had to be Zelan. I turned around, but it was only Golen not Zelan. "Right, I do think it is time for me to head off to bed. Alone. Good night, gentlemen. This was an… interesting evening." It really was fun and made me realize that I wasn't cut out for flirting with lots of guys. If they wanted to be friends, I could do that. Anything more would not be welcomed.

"Natalie, I must warn you. Warriors who have found their mate tend to be very territorial. Which is why my people have made it a rule to never mess with another's mate. Wars have started over it in the past. Please keep that in mind next time you want to have some fun." Golen had his hand on my shoulder and was guiding me out the door.

"I know. I didn't realize that they would be so intense. It was just supposed to be some light flirting and fun, nothing more. None of those guys wanted me as their mate. They were just looking for a way to blow off some steam. It was harmless." I bit my lip as I thought about Zelan and what he would have thought if he had walked in to see all those guys surrounding me. Even I knew he wouldn't like it.

"Golen, are your kind very promiscuous?" I hadn't met too many of these guys, and so far I had seen several guys flash red when they looked at me. I wasn't ugly, but I also wasn't going to win any Miss Universe pageants. Wow, how ethnocentric are we as a people to think that we were the only ones in the universe? That pageant means something totally different to me now.

"What do you mean?" He continued to walk facing forward and had his hands behind his back.

"Well, I have only met a few of your males, and already

several of them have had red flashing veins in my presence. I got the feeling that they wanted more than to just kiss my cheek. Is that normal with your kind?" I fidgeted with my hands, not really comfortable with this conversation. However, it was necessary.

Zelan came around the corner. "There you are, Natalie. The Commander told me I should go get you and take you home tonight. That you were stranded in the mess hall with a room full of single, male warriors. Are you alright?" He walked up to me and grabbed me in a tight hug.

To be honest, I was a bit happy to see him. He had never been anything but a gentleman with me. Not once did I feel weird with him. The hug felt right, like a friend comforting someone they thought was upset, which I wasn't. Although, it was welcome.

"I'm fine. Golen was walking me back to Paris' place. How was work?" I was still wrapped in his arms, but it felt nice.

Golen cleared his throat. "I will be heading to bed now. Captain, I take it you will see that Natalie gets back safely?"

"Hm, oh, yes. I will take her home. Thank you for looking out for her safety tonight. I owe you one." Zelan put his hand on my low back. It felt much nicer than when Golen put his hand on my shoulder. It was like all was right in the world. Zelan even had his purple veins again. They really did relax me. I wondered why.

"Zelan, why is it that I feel so much better when your veins pulse purple? Is that some sort of calming effect of the color?" I had an idea but wanted to hear what he had to say.

He smiled at me, and then leaned down and kissed the top of my head. "It just means that you are responding to the bond which is forming between us. As mates grow closer, they become more in tune with each other's emotions. Since you are human, your emotions won't affect me nearly as much. But my emotions will affect you. Over time, you will come to understand exactly what I am feeling. At times you will feel the same as me unless your emotions are stronger than mine. When that happens, your emotions will rule you." He pressed his palm into my back a little bit more, and it was quite relaxing.

"Hmm, that's very strange. I think I have felt it happen a few times already. One time you were pulsing blue, and I was sad that your purple veins were gone. I thought it was just because I love the color purple. I didn't realize I was picking up on your sad emotions. Doesn't that get in the way of doing your job?"

"Sometimes, but this way there is no fooling each other. It is very important for a leader to understand those serving under him. We can better lead when we understand our crew or team. Sometimes words aren't even necessary. It works quite well, for the most part."

We walked up to my door and stopped in front of it. "Thank you for walking me home. Will I see you tomorrow? I understand you have a busy day with sending troops over to New Hope." I put my hand on his arm and felt a bit flustered when my hand touched his bare arm. His muscles flexed and I felt the raw strength in him and could feel my face heating up. I only hoped he couldn't see my blush.

Ben didn't really have any muscles, at least none on this level. I hated to admit it to myself, but I was a little bit turned on. Who knew I was a muscle girl? At least my veins weren't pulsing red. That would have been embarrassing.

I looked up into his eyes and felt an intense connection. Was he going to kiss me? Did I want him to? At that moment, I did want him to. Although it would send the wrong message if I allowed that, so I stepped back closer to the door.

He cleared his throat and said, "I will try to see you tomorrow if at all possible. Maybe we could have dinner tomorrow night?"

"Yes," I looked down at my feet not wanting him to see my blush. "I would like that. Call me if you can make it. Otherwise, I'll just eat with Paris." I leaned in to give him a hug goodnight. Friends did that sort of thing all the time. There shouldn't be any mixed signals with a hug. Right?

He whispered in my ear, "Goodnight, my Natalie." Then he leaned down and kissed my cheek. At that moment, I wanted nothing more than for him to push me up against the wall and kiss the dickens out of me. An extreme need for him filled my entire body, and I almost threw him against the wall. If not for the small voice in the back of my head that said *don't do it,* I might have.

He stepped away from me and walked backward a few steps looking intently into my eyes, before he turned around and walked way. I was left breathing heavily and wondering what just happened. Was that the mating bond he was talking about? These next few months were going to be torture if I succumbed to it.

CHAPTER THIRTEEN

"Ugh, what is that noise?" I moaned. It had to be the middle of the night still. I lifted my head and looked toward the noise. In the kitchen, I saw Commander Venay had pinned Paris against the wall. "Oh, my word! It's way too early to see that." I took my pillow and covered my head.

I didn't get back to sleep until he left for work. When I did wake up, Paris was in the kitchen drinking tea. The V'Zenian tea was good, but I couldn't wait until I got to the settlement and had real, Earth coffee again.

It was strange; I would normally call things American and was very ethnocentric when it came to what I liked. *Made in America* was a big deal to my family. But then again, my dad did run a business in America.

Now, I would take Columbian or Ugandan coffee any day. It didn't have to be packaged by an American company either. Anything from Earth would be wonderful.

It would be nice to socialize with humans from different parts of my world too. I wondered if I would get that chance. How many on this planet were from other parts of my world?

"Good morning, Paris. I was just thinking how nice it

would be to have some Earth coffee again. Is it strange that I'm actually looking forward to going back to that settlement? Even after the attack?" I fixed myself some hot tea and sat at the table with her.

"Actually, it isn't strange at all. While it is an alien outpost on a distant planet, so much of it felt like Earth. I hope that I get to go there often as well. Maybe even pick up some coffee to bring back here. Did you want any breakfast? I'm feeling very domesticated lately and could make you scrambled eggs and bacon with toast if you like."

I giggled. "Paris, all it takes is the push of a button to make that. It isn't really *cooking* when you use the replicator." I shook my head at her silliness.

"No, I suppose not. But, humor me. This is the closest I will get to cooking. Last night Venay told me that we will most likely be heading straight to the border with the Zateelians when his new ship arrives. Their President is in talks right now with their version of a war council, and it looks like they are preparing to go to war with the mutant cockroaches." She sighed and took a sip of her tea.

"Oh, I am sorry to hear that. I know you wanted to head to their planet to try and change things for us humans. What does that mean for us? Will we get to stay on this planet?"

"Most likely. Although, since we are going to be here for so long, Venay thinks that a lot of his warriors will find their mates here. So, you could end up on the ship with us. As could a lot of our friends. All the human men will stay here. Hopefully, they'll fall in line and accept their jobs and be happy. There are quite a lot of human women on this planet. Maybe they'll even find wives, settle down, and raise families." She shrugged her shoulders.

What more could she ask for those who were abducted with us? There was no way the V'Zenians were going to return any of us to Earth. The next best thing would be to leave us all here where we would have some freedoms and a chance to make something of this colony.

"I hope I get to stay here. I know that you guys are expecting me to mate with Zelan." I sighed and shrugged. "Maybe part of me wants that too, I really don't know. But I do know that I want to stay here. This is the next best thing to going home. Please don't be upset with me." I looked up at her and quirked a small smile. "Can you understand that?"

She reached across the table and grabbed my hand, "Of course I can. Maybe this is your calling. I know what mine is. Staying with Venay, wherever he goes is what I am called to do. Whenever I get the chance to help humans, you better believe I will. And that means accepting when they find their place, even if it isn't where I want them to be." Paris let go of my hand and got up to fix my breakfast.

"You have become a great friend over these past couple of weeks. Geez, I can't believe it's only been a couple of weeks since we left Earth. Time has really flown by. So much has happened." I sighed and thought about how much I've changed since my abduction.

"If you know where you belong, then fight for it. That is all I can ask of any of my friends." She smiled over her shoulder as she pushed the buttons on the replicator.

"Thank you. I feel the same way. You are more like a sister than a friend. I want you to know how much I truly appreciate you looking out for me," I honestly stated.

"That is what friends do. Okay, enough of that mushy stuff." We both smirked. "Natalie, what do you want to do today?"

"I think I want to visit with Sheila and the rest of the mated girls. See how they're all doing and find out who else is going to the settlement. Also, is there any way to get there sooner? Not that I want to leave you, but they have chocolate chip pancakes and coffee!" I was practically drooling thinking about the Earth foods I used to take for granted. My stomach growled its own desire for chocolate chip pancakes.

Paris opened her eyes wide and then drew out a long WOW. "That's right! They really do have chocolate chip pancakes. Do they taste just as good as home?"

"Our last morning in the colony Zelan took me there for breakfast. They use a different type of milk, which makes them richer. But man, are they ever good!" I licked my lips thinking about how good they were.

"Hmm, maybe we should take a trip tomorrow to scout out the living arrangements. You know, so we can prepare the girls for where they are going to go? And of course, check out a couple of their diners, just to get an idea of what life will be like there." She rubbed her hands together, and I could tell she was dreaming of those pancakes, too.

"It's amazing how something so simple becomes so big when you no longer have it at your disposal, isn't it? I did a study abroad to Estonia when I was in college. They didn't have pancake mix or chocolate chips like what we have. I had to make it from scratch. Thankfully, my mom had email and she sent me the recipe. Then I went and found a couple of large chocolate bars. I broke them up into small pieces and used them in place of the chocolate chips." I got up and went over to the counter and picked up my breakfast that Paris so graciously made for me.

"Estonia didn't have any maple syrup. I met a mission-ary's wife who was from the mid-west and she made her own syrup. It wasn't the same, but you have no idea how good those pancakes were! I was going through culture shock and those really helped me to have a piece of home. Well, that and I went to Mickey D's a few times a week for lunch. I think our situation here is like that, but a thousand times worse. Since we aren't even on planet Earth." I chewed on the side of my lower lip as I thought about all that I had experienced on this trip so far. It was so far above anything I had ever seen in my short life on Earth.

"I never left the states but living on the streets did bring some culture shock with it. At first, it was all about staying safe. I had to learn to sleep with one eye open to make sure that no one ever got the drop on me. Then I had to learn how to make friends." Paris made herself another cup of tea before she went back to the table.

"I thought that other women would be good companions on the street, but it turned out the same issues with cattiness are a part of life on the streets as they are in high school. Most of the older men made better friends. Which was weird since the oldest man I ever knew was my dad. Those guys on the streets were older than he was when he died. Making friends here has been much easier, though. I guess that's one good thing." She shrugged her shoulders.

I thought about her experience before responding, "I think part of it is that you are mated to the head honcho. Everyone wants to be your friend. Not that I like you for your status. I don't work that way. There are some women here who do, so be careful who you befriend. Especially watch out for a girl named Rachelle. She is a social climber if I ever saw one. She's after Zelan, but he doesn't seem to want her attentions."

That brought a laugh out of Paris. "Of course not, he only has eyes for one woman. Thank you for the warning. I'll be careful."

We were both quiet for the rest of our breakfast. I thought about the concept of culture shock and realized we were all probably going through that in our various ways. I knew from my own experience the best way to get through it without going crazy was to find things that reminded us of home and experience them. We also had to come to grips with our situation as it was. If we didn't accept our fate and move forward, a lot of us would end up going batty.

Not that we had to roll-over and just accept the first male to want us or agree to be slaves. We could, and should, do whatever we could in our power to make our lives better. What I realized was that Paris had it right, we needed to accept we weren't ever going home. It was time I looked to my future and stopped complaining about my past, or even my present situation.

I did have options. What I needed to do was think about them and figure out what I wanted for myself in this new reality. Did I want to mate with Zelan? Did I want a mate at all? Family was something I had always wanted. But, now that I was on an alien world, did that mean the same thing here?

My current situation was so completely different from anything I had ever fantasized about. I needed time to acclimate to my new surroundings and re-adjust my wants and dreams. I only hoped Zelan would give me that time.

After we got ready, I went with Paris to help feed all of our people. I discovered that pretty much all of them were on the list to get their universal translators installed. "Lucy, when do you get your translator implanted?"

"First thing tomorrow morning. Both Betty and I are on the list! I'm so excited. That means we get to be part of the early group to head out to the colony. What's it like? Will we all get real rooms? Or just a bigger cell?" Lucy's eyes were bright, and she had a huge smile plastered on her face. She seemed to be very excited about everything. I hoped she would enjoy her time in the settlement.

Several of the women had moved closer to where we were so they could hear the conversation.

"I don't know for sure, but from what I've heard, we will all live in barracks. So, we will share a large room with other women, but it won't be a jail cell. We can come and go as we please, and everyone will get a job. They have restaurants too! The best part is they have coffee from Earth! I can't wait to go." I sighed dreamily as I remembered the taste of their coffee and the pungent aroma of the arabica beans as they brewed.

Rachelle was in the cell next to us and she asked, "Where's Zelan? I haven't seen him for a couple of days. He promised to come visit me."

I gave Rachelle a tight smile and tried to hide my frustration with the wench. "He's very busy now that he was promoted to Captain. He'll be overseeing all the warriors the Commander is sending with us to the colony. It's his responsibility to train them, along with the other warriors already residing there, to defend the place against the bugs."

"Really, he's a Captain now? I suppose that means you are going to go after him? Just remember, I wanted him when he was a lowly Lieutenant. I don't care about rank. He should be my mate." Rachelle looked at me with a scowl on her face.

I couldn't believe she really thought she should have him. A week ago, I would have said, *Go for it*. Now, it's more like, *Stay away, he's mine*. I think I understand why Paris fell so fast for the Commander. However, I wasn't going to do that. Like I said before, I was going to take it slow and date the guy before I decided anything more.

"Actually, I think I met just the right guy for you last night. His name is Zelion, and he has a twin brother named Maximillian. They are both here and going to the colony this week. Zel is a real flirt, and Max is a total sweety. You might be able to have them both if you play your cards right." I almost rolled my eyes thinking about her with Max. I bet he wouldn't give her the time of day. But if telling her she had a chance at both meant keeping her away from Zelan, then it was worth it.

"Oh, really? Twins? Hm, that might be a lot of fun. I guess I could meet them and see what they're like." She was a piece of work.

Lucy and Betty tried really hard to stifle their giggles but lost that battle. "Natalie, really? Trying to get her to go for two other men? I take it you've decided to go for Zelan after all?" Betty asked.

"Well, Zelan and I are dating." I felt my cheeks heat and prayed no one noticed. "We're going to spend time getting to know each other. That is all. No mating going on here. But he is off the market. I don't want anyone else trying to take him away. At least, not until I'm sure what I want."

"Uh huh, you keep telling yourself that's all it is. I bet by next month you two are mated and living together in utter bliss, just like Paris and the Commander." Lucy's smile was a mile wide.

I waved at them both. "Whatever. I just want the chance to get to know him, that's all."

Paris came over and said it was time to go if I wanted to spend time with my other friends today. So we left and went to see Sheila first.

"Sheila!" I yelled and ran to give her a hug. "It's so good to see you again. How is mated life? Is Cazon treating you good?"

She returned my hug. "Natalie, it's great to see you again. I hear you're leaving us soon. To live in the colony? And with that hunk of an alien, Zelan. Nice job!" She wiggled her eyebrows up and down.

"Oh, stop it! Not you too! Does Paris have everyone in on this or what? Even the Commander is trying to get us together." I crossed my arms over my chest and shifted my weight to my left leg.

"Come on. You have to admit that mating with these aliens is pretty awesome. Have you two consummated anything yet?" Sheila was going to get slapped if she didn't stop it.

I hated discussing sex with anyone, especially with people I hardly knew.

"No, he hasn't even kissed me yet. Well, not anywhere

except for my cheek. Which is exactly the way I want it." It was, wasn't it?

"Oh, sweetie, you are missing out! I never knew what I was missing until I mated with Cazon. He is..."

I interrupted her right there.

"TMI! TMI! I don't need to hear the details of your love life." I put my hands up in front of my head and turned my face towards the ground like that was going to block her words from me.

"You did ask how I was doing. That is pretty much all I am doing these days if you get my meaning." Sheila winked and nudged my shoulder.

"Ugh, can we please change the subject? How is Lisa? Is she happy with Rotna?" Why did I want to see mated girls? I had to remember to stop talking to them. All they had on their mind was one thing.

Sheila laughed and offered us seats. "Yes, she's on her way here now. You can ask her yourself."

We spent the rest of the day catching up, and I told them all about my harrowing adventures since we moved to this ship. Rotna was considering moving to the settlement as well. I hoped they did so I could at least have one friend. Well, as long as Lisa didn't try to tell me about her sex life or try to get me to mate with Zelan. I needed a friend who would understand what I was going through and support me.

Zelan called me late that afternoon to confirm that I would have dinner with him. To be honest, I was looking forward to it. Which was strange. When I was dating Ben, I didn't get chills thinking about our dates. Excitement wasn't part of my life back then. Now that I thought about it, it was more resignation than anything else that I felt when I would get ready for a date with Ben.

Life had really changed a lot in the course of a few weeks.

I didn't have any clothes other than what I was given after

my shower at Paris' place the other day, which was a type of cargo pants and a t-shirt, so I wasn't able to get all dolled up for him. However, he did have a nice pair of denim jeans on with an iridescent blue button up shirt. The pants were from Earth, but that shirt, it must have been from his planet. It contoured his body perfectly. The cuffs of his sleeves were rolled up to his biceps and stretched taut, showing off his muscles. I was practically salivating thinking about them.

"Natalie, did you want to have dinner in my quarters or in the mess hall?" He put his hand out for mine, and I gladly gave it to him. He took my hand and put it inside the crook of his arm, and we walked out of my temporary quarters.

"Would you mind if we ate in the mess hall? I am not a big fan of the V'Zenian menus." I also didn't want to be alone with the giant alien in his quarters. Not that I thought he would try anything untoward, but I didn't want to give him the idea that I would be open to any such activities.

"Of course, I should have thought about that."

"No worries. Once we are at New Hope, it shouldn't be an issue, right? I mean they have lots of human food in their restaurants and most likely in their replicators, right?" I hadn't thought about anything other than the coffee corner, pancake place, and the ice cream parlor. They had to have plenty of other human food too, right?

"I know they have a few little restaurants that serve your food, but they aren't open all the time. Maybe with the new influx of humans they can be open more often. Although, I don't know where they get their food from. We bring them items from Earth each trip. That can't last very long. And this trip what food we scavenged from our old ship was brought to this one for all of you. I guess you will just have to wait and be surprised." He patted my hand where it laid.

I squeezed his arm in response and smiled. "Another adventure? As long as we don't see any more of those bugs, I'll be just fine."

"I am not sure they have been exterminated yet. That is partly why so many warriors are going with us. There is no need to worry, with two hundred extra trained fighters, you will be safe. Stay alert, and never leave the safety of the walls without a security force accompanying you, and you won't have anything to worry about." We arrived at the mess hall, and it was crowded. There weren't any empty tables.

We walked toward the replicators, and I noticed Balin and Eshen, they were at a table with a few others I didn't recognize. "Hi guys, how goes it?" I waved to them. They timidly waved back and gave me very small smiles. I felt Zelan stiffen when he looked at them. "What's wrong?"

"How do you know them?" He nodded towards the table of guys.

"They were here last night when we had our movie night. They were nice and polite. Nothing to worry about." I nudged his arm with my shoulder.

"One of them seems very attracted to you," he said gruffly.

"Zelan, I'm on a date with you, not him. So don't worry. I think they all got the hint when the Commander announced that you had claimed me as your mate." I shook my head.

He whipped his head toward me. "He said that? Really? To all of the men in here last night?"

"Yes, he did. Anyone who was sitting anywhere near me moved. Didn't you see how they greeted me tonight? They were worried you'd be upset. So give them a break and realize that I will be making friends with the guys on your team. It's not like there are thousands of people here. We're going to add significantly to the size of the outpost when we all move over there, aren't we?" I looked at the menu selections on the replicator while meathead next to me thought about what I said.

"They really did move away once they heard you were taken?" He smiled and put his hand on the small of my back.

"Look, I'm a one-man kind of woman. I said I wanted to date you, and I do. That's what we're doing tonight. Golen did warn me about you." I sighed. "I won't date anyone else while we're dating. I understand that alien males can't handle jealousy well, so stop flashing black and look at me instead of those guys who are cowering under your glare." I grabbed his chin and pulled it towards me. "I don't like jealousy. It's a stupid emotion, so check it at the door when we are together. Got it?"

He was so infuriating. That smile of his was so bright it could light the room all on its own. Add to it the fact that he pulsed purple again, and I knew he was excited about what I just said. Alien men were so strange.

"You are right, Natalie. I am sorry. Sometimes it is very difficult for V'Zenian's to not get jealous. It is a failing that we all deal with. What would you like for dinner?" He looked at the replicator menu as I scrolled through it.

"I think a nice baked chicken breast with rice sounds really good. What about you? Do you have any favorites?" It was time to get to know each other. I read once in Cosmo that you should know what your man loves to eat. The way to his heart was through his stomach or some such nonsense. I wondered if it was the same with aliens.

"My favorite meal is the Gardorzch. I think the closest Earth meal would be beef stew. I love mine with the green vegetables. We have a hearty one that looks similar to your Kale. Do you like Kale?" My meal had just come out, and he was selecting his.

"Not really. Vegetables are not all that tasty to me. I prefer meat and potatoes or rice. Although, I do love salads and corn. Back home I took vitamins to make up for my lack of vegetables." I took my plate and looked around for a table. None were open. "Should we take this back to your place? All of the tables are full."

He turned around and gave a menacing stare to the guys I

spoke to earlier, and they all got up immediately and left the room. "That wasn't very nice. It's not like there's another place they can go to have fun inside of this ship."

"Yes, there is. This ship is equipped with a full-size gym. That is why the holding cells are so small. Normally, our ships have a nice gym and even a running track. So they have plenty to do besides taking up space in the mess hall, especially since they have already eaten." He picked his plate up from the replicator, and I followed him to the newly vacated table.

As soon as we sat down, the tables directly next to us also emptied out rather quickly. A couple of the men hadn't even finished their meals. Instead, they ate standing up next to the far wall.

"Why did they do that? They could have stayed here." I shook my head.

"Because they realized that we needed privacy. They probably assumed we would be discussing our mating. You might get some questions once we relocate to New Hope as to why you are living in the barracks and not with me. I support whatever you wish to say." His soft voice sent goosebumps all down my arms, until I realized what he was really saying.

"Seriously? People are going to ask why I haven't jumped into bed with you yet? We only just met. That's crazy. Surely not everyone moves as fast as the Commander, Rotna, and Cazon?" Or *was* that the norm?

"Those relationships moved at the normal pace for a human and a VZ Hybrid. Since I am full-blooded, we should have already mated. Normally the process is faster as our emotions are stronger. I am curious why you have not yet succumbed to my emotions. While I have kept them in check to the best of my abilities, you should be feeling a very strong pull to me." He furrowed his brow and looked at me.

It was rather disconcerting.

"I... well, um, I do have strong feelings for you. Nonetheless, I have stronger feelings about maintaining my identity while I figure this all out. You did say you would give me time. Did you think that by saying something like that I would be appeased, and it would only take a few days for me to fall into your arms?" I pointed my fork at him and then narrowed one eye.

"No, I...well I did think it wouldn't take you long to realize the attraction and become ready for me." He squirmed in his seat.

It was about time he felt some nerves over this entire situation. Since I met him he has been in charge and control to some degree. I finally had the upper hand.

A slow smile spread across my face. "Zelan, I meant what I said. We have five months to figure this out. I plan on taking that time. All of it. So don't think that I will be in your arms within the week. Maybe it will happen before the new ship arrives, and maybe not."

His eyes opened wide and his veins turned blue. "Five months? You want to wait that long?"

I sighed. "Zelan, we barely know each other. I have no idea if we even have the same beliefs about family and where we are going to live. This takes time. We need a chance to get to know one another better and see if we really are compatible. I want something more than just strong emotions, I want a true friendship and partnership with the man I'm going to marry.

He took my hand in his and his face softened when he looked me in the eyes. "Natalie, I want the same thing. The only reason I came on this mission was to find a mate so I could have children. We both agree on family and how important it is. The rest will come in time. We will have the rest of our lives to get to know one another deeply. I want you with me before we leave this planet."

"Honestly, I was hoping to stay here. What were your

plans? To join the Commander and head back to Earth so you could abduct more humans?" I pulled my hand from his, sat back, and crossed my arms over my chest and scowled.

"Actually, yes. I thought you would come around like Paris has and be happy on our ship. You have friends here. However, the plans have recently changed. We are to head to the border with the Zateelians. Even if we don't go to war, we still have to show them our strength. They can't get away with what they have done here." His veins started to pulse orange, which meant he was getting upset.

"Our President is livid over the attack. This planet is too far inside our space. They should never have come this far, and the fact that they have sent several ships here to attack us just means they want war." He put his fork down and looked off into the distance.

"I am sure we are talking to our allies right now and getting the assistance we will need to rid the universe of those disgusting, mutant cockroaches. They don't even deserve to breathe the same air as us." He pounded his hand on the table and his veins began to pulse black.

This conversation had gone way off target.

"I agree, they need to be exterminated like the slimy bugs they are. Can we turn this conversation back to something nicer? Like New Hope? I like that name it really does represent what I'm feeling right now, hope. Hope for a brighter future. Maybe even one that includes us… here… together." I took hold of his hand, squeezed it, and smiled tentatively for him. He needed to calm down and showing him affection usually helped to turn his veins back to purple.

"Thank you, Natalie. This is why I need you in my life, even if you aren't my mate, yet. You have the power to calm me down. No one else can do that for a V'Zenian. Especially for a pure-blood. We tend to fly off the handle a bit faster than the hybrids." He interlocked our fingers together and moved so that we were sitting next to each other instead of across from one another.

That overwhelming desire to kiss him took hold of me, and I couldn't stop it. Right there in the mess hall, in front of all who were left in the room, I kissed Zelan. It was our first real kiss. I swear I saw fireworks. He pulled me tight against his chest and wrapped his strong arms around me. I grabbed ahold of his biceps and held on for my life. Ben never kissed me like that.

Our lips fit together perfectly and his tongue, oh my! His tongue knew exactly what to do. Mine even responded in a way I had never experienced before. My heart was pounding so loud I thought for sure it was going to jump out of my chest. If I died right there, I would have been a very happy woman.

Without breaking the kiss, he picked me up and pushed me up against the wall, just as I imagined yesterday. I don't know how he knew it was what I wanted, but he did. His hands were all over my sides, and one even grabbed my butt. I think I moaned when he did that. I should have been embarrassed, but I wasn't thinking clearly. Obviously.

My hands roamed along his arms and then over his chest. Oh, that chest, I knew that once I accepted his offer, he would never be allowed to wear a shirt when we were alone. I wanted to take his shirt off right then and there until I realized where we were and what I was doing. I gently pushed back against his chest and pulled my head back from him just a bit. He got the message and ended the kiss. He did not pull away from me. Instead, he was breathing very heavily and put his forehead against mine.

"Natalie, please don't be mad at me. That was the best kiss I have ever experienced." He kissed me on the temple, and I almost kissed him back.

"I'm not mad. It was getting a bit too intense for me. And from what I can see of your veins, for you as well." I was breathing heavily just like he was. However, his veins were pulsing a very deep red, almost burgundy.

He kissed my cheek and the corner of my lips. "I agree. That was very intense. Too bad our first official kiss was in front of a crowd." He lightly chuckled as he kissed my neck under my ear.

I moved my head and finally noticed that the room was completely cleared out. "When did everyone leave?"

He turned his head and scanned the room. "Pretty much as soon as I picked you up and pushed you up against the wall. Not that I was paying them any attention. Nevertheless, I did hear the chairs scrape against the floor as everyone made a hasty retreat." He went back to kissing my neck, which was giving me goosebumps all over my body and sent shivers down my spine.

My breathing started to get heavy again, and my mouth looked for his. For the second time, I initiated the kissing.

After a couple of minutes, he asked, "Do you want to go back to my room?" Then he trailed kisses down the side of my neck to my collarbone.

"Yes. I mean no. I'm not ready for that yet." I pushed back against his chest again, and this time, I put my forehead on his chest to keep him from kissing me again.

He kissed the top of my head. "I understand." He hugged me tightly before pulling back. "Are you still hungry or do you want to do something else?"

"I'm not really hungry, but I should probably eat some of my dinner. I only took a couple of bites." I chuckled and felt my cheeks heat. In fact, my entire body was hot. That kiss was unlike anything I had ever experienced before. Was it because Zelan's an alien? Or was it as he said, we were fated mates? If I kissed another alien would it feel like that?

We went back to our meals and ate quietly. I couldn't get that kiss out of my head. His hands, oh goodness! They felt so good on my body. It never felt like this with Ben.

Ben rarely touched me. Thinking back now, I wondered how I never realized that he wasn't interested in me physically.

Once I was finished with my dinner, I asked him to take me home.

"Which home? Mine, or Paris'?"

I chuckled. "Paris' quarters please. I won't be sharing your bed until we are mated."

"So that means you have decided to accept my proposal?" His eyelids hooded an he stared at my mouth.

"Um, not yet. I don't doubt that it will happen, but I still need some time. We need to figure out where we are going to live. Honestly, I want to stay here on the planet." I was so excited to move to New Hope and start a life there, I couldn't even think about going back to space.

His smile started to fade a little. "I don't know if that is possible for me. But like you said, we still have five months. Maybe Commander Croso will request that I stay on once the battalion of warriors arrives."

We got up and cleaned our dishes, and he walked me back to my quarters. "Goodnight, Zelan. I hope you didn't get the wrong idea when I kissed you tonight. Truly, I don't know what came over me. It was an overwhelming need to kiss you and be closer to you that I couldn't fight." I could feel my cheeks burning as I admitted to him how I felt.

He kissed my cheek and pulled back. "I think those might have been my feelings you picked up on. I have been fighting my desire for you over this past week but most especially since our time at New Hope. Please forgive me if my emotions took control of you." He sheepishly looked down at our feet.

I pulled his chin up. "It's fine. I really did enjoy that kiss. In fact, I hope that our next date is soon so I can kiss you like that again. Just, maybe not quite so intense the next time. Or public."

He gave me a chaste kiss on the lips that lingered just enough to make me want more. "Goodnight, sweet dreams. I will comm you tomorrow as soon as I get some time." He kissed me again on the top of my head and stood back and waited until I went inside Paris' quarters.

CHAPTER FOURTEEN

The next morning when I woke up, I was already missing Zelan. My dreams were full of him, and this morning I ached to have him hold me. What was wrong with me?

I got up and found Paris in the kitchen. She had just finished her breakfast. "Paris, I need to ask you some personal stuff." I fixed myself some tea and sat down at the table. She joined me. "When you first accepted the Commander's proposal to be his mate, you were not yet attracted to him, right?"

"True, but once we started spending time together my attraction grew rather quickly. It seemed a bit supernatural in its intensity and speed. I quickly accepted it and haven't looked back once. There are some issues I still have to deal with, but I suppose it's the same for you?"

"Yes, the slavery issue is the biggest concern I have. That being said, I also really wanted to spend some time getting to know who I am as a person. Not as someone else's plus one." I sighed and wondered what had happened to staying single for a while. "I have seen women who go from man to man, never understanding who they are as a woman. That's not what I want."

"You're feeling the pull, aren't you? To mate with Zelan?" Paris was trying to hide her smile, but I could see the corners of her mouth tilted up and her cheeks begin to color.

"Yes, he kissed me for the first time last night. Actually, it was me who kissed him." I looked down at the cup in my hands and chucked. "But the desire was so strong it seemed to control me. I pretty much attacked him in the mess hall in front of a bunch of warriors. Thankfully, they cleared the room pretty quickly." I shook my head remembering last night.

"I wish I could have seen that. Zelan must have been in heaven." She smiled over the rim of her teacup.

"Yes, he was rather pleased. He told me that my emotions probably came from him. It seems that as a pure-blood, his emotions will control me more than a hybrid's would. That scares me a little. Are my feelings for him real, or is it just his emotions taking over mine? It doesn't make sense." If my emotions weren't my own, then there was no way I could marry him.

"I had a similar situation with Venay, and he explained it to me that my emotions are real. His emotions can heighten mine, but he can't actually create emotions within me that aren't already there. So, that means that you do have real feelings for Zelan. I didn't realize that a pure-blood could influence you more than a hybrid. That's very interesting." She chewed on her lower lip as she considered the situation.

"So, does that mean I do have real feelings for him and his abilities are just heightening them? Or does he have the ability to create feelings in me that I wouldn't naturally have? You know, since he's a pureblood?" If he could create emotions in me, that really scared me. However, if he was just able to heighten what I already felt for him, well ... I wasn't sure how I felt about that, not yet anyway.

"It's something you'll want to keep in mind. Be sure to set your boundaries with him. He seems to be very honorable and I doubt he would push you to go further than you're willing to, but he needs to know exactly what you do and don't want. In a way, it's refreshing. There is no need to play games with these men. Be honest and upfront and they will respect you for it. Plus, he'll know when to stop."

"Thank you, Paris. That really helps. I can't believe you can't come with me. I'm going to miss you. I know that sounds weird, but I really value your opinion. Plus, you and Lisa were the first ones to take the plunge. Sheila, well, she went in cannon ball style so her experiences are very different." We both chuckled thinking back to how that woman flirted so hard with so many of the warriors in the beginning. She was the only one I have met so far who was excited to be abducted.

"Glad I could help. Now, I think today might be a good day to head over to the settlement and check out the living situation for everyone. What do you think?" Paris asked with a grin.

"Paris, I couldn't agree more. Let's do this!" I was very excited to see where I was going to live and to meet more of the residents of New Hope. If all went well, this would be the place I would live out the rest of my life.

I never thought I'd be excited to live in such a small place before. Malls and coffee shops and parks were always a part of my life. I guess, there is a coffee shop and one of the largest parks ever imagined is just outside the settlement walls. Maybe I could survive without a mall. Actually, I knew I could survive without shopping. In fact, this was the first time I had even though about shopping since being abducted. Huh? I wondered what that meant.

By lunch time we were at the settlement. Commander Venay and Zelan came with us. We all hitched a ride with the warriors who were being transferred there.

"Haver, Aysiaer, it's good to see the two of you again. I hope you are enjoying all of the extra flights you have scheduled this week." I shook their hands when I entered and Aysiaer held mine a bit too long. He released my hand when Zelan growled.

That was the first time I'd heard him do that. He reminded me of an alpha shifter from one of my favorite books back home. Which reminded me, we were going to have to get a list of items together so that next time someone went to Earth we could get some supplies, like a great collection of books.

Aysiaer moved away immediately while Haver chuckled and shook his head. "Yes, it has been a nice change of pace flying back and forth. Yesterday, we even went out on a recon flight to look for that crashed ship. I hope we can find any last hideouts by those insectoids and destroy them all."

"I have to agree with you there. Don't you have a satellite system in orbit to help you track them?" Even we had such technology back on Earth. Surely these advanced aliens had even better tech than us backward humans did.

"No, we have a weather satellite, and one to relay messages to our other planets, but nothing that will help us to track down any crashed ships or find living beings outside of our settlement." Haver looked to Zelan and then back to me and I wondered if an unspoken message had passed between them.

The Commander boarded at that point. "We actually have one on the way, Natalie. I think it might be time you set up your office and get up to speed on what we have going on here. Zelan, I want her on tomorrow's shipment of warriors to the settlement. Today we need to find her space to live and work. There is much to do."

"Commander, thank you. Not that I don't appreciate you letting me sleep on your couch, but it would be nice to have somewhere else to sleep." Mentally I added, *somewhere that doesn't have two newlyweds waking me up early in the morning with their lovemaking.*

"Yes, I am sure. Alright Haver, if we have everything let's get moving. I have a lot to do today," the Commander barked out.

Haver moved to his seat in the front of the ship. "Yes, sir!"

It was a nice flight to the settlement. Zelan and I chatted about nothing in particular. It wasn't exactly the place to talk about personal stuff. Even if we had whispered, all of the warriors had excellent hearing, they would have heard it all.

Captain Mypo was waiting for us when we arrived. "Natalie, if you will follow me, I will show you to the women's barracks. There aren't many living there right now so you will have your pick of the place." The imposing female warrior was still the only one I had seen so far on this planet. Maybe the Captain was an anomaly? Or maybe since this planet was so small, she just happened to be the only female warrior. Just one more item to add to my list of questions.

Paris and I both followed her. She was right, it was mostly open. Only two other women had set up bunks in the place. There was room for another twenty women in this one room alone. "There are six other bunk houses if you don't like this one. However, it is the closest one to your new office."

"I'll take it. How long before some more apartments open up?" I could live here, but I really wanted some privacy for a change.

The Captain walked around the large open bay with a total of twenty-two bunks and wardrobes. "We weren't planning on giving any of you an apartment yet. It is best to wait and see what happens first. Many women will mate with our warriors, and some will leave."

"Do you have a place where we can get more clothes? I only have what I'm wearing plus a change of undergarments. The warriors on our ship didn't plan on us changing our clothes often." Or all, from what I could tell.

"There is a factory that makes clothes here. They could use some more bodies. Do you know if anyone in your group can sew? We really need more workers to handle the influx of warriors and people. There is also a need for trained cooks." Captain Mypo led us back outside as we headed towards the industrial area.

"I will have to talk to everyone to see what they specialize in. That might be a great first project for me unless the Commander has something else in mind. He did say he needed me to move here tomorrow and get up to speed. I'll have to ask him what he had in mind." I couldn't believe I already had a project needing my attention. Maybe life on this planet wouldn't be so bad. It would be nice to stay busy and contribute to the settlement.

Once we made it to the factory, my measurements were taken, and I was told that I would have a full set of clothes by the end of the week. They were going to send over to my room a couple changes of clothes and undergarments I could use until my new ones were completed.

"There will be a long line once everyone moves here, won't there?" Paris asked.

The Captain responded, "Yes, it is good Natalie is here early. We might want to send a couple of seamstresses to the ship just to get some measurements so we can get started. Natalie, do you want to handle that as well?"

"Sure, I'll get with Zelan to see when we have a transport with room going back to the ship." I could feel the stress leaving my body, which was strange. You'd think I'd be more stressful with all the responsibilities piling up. But this was what I wanted, to feel needed in a way that made a differ-ence. Back home, I only felt as though I was an ornament on Ben's arm. Not that he needed me, or anyone else did for any reason other than to help Ben look good.

Here, on Zeleron 10, I was going to help humans adapt to their new environment and quite possibly help an alien race to view humans as more than cattle.

The rest of the day was spent looking at offices with the

Commander and Zelan. They were able to choose where they wanted to work, and I was given a desk next to their offices. It was a very spacious area, and no one else was in this section of the building. It was nice and private. But that also meant that our coffee corner wasn't stocked yet. That was something I needed to get on right away.

When we went back down to the lobby, I saw Clarissa. "Hi there, looks like we will be working together soon. I can't wait to move here tomorrow. But I gotta ask, how do I get a coffee corner set up on our floor?"

She smiled at me. "I'll take care of that. Since we had no plans to put anyone there yet, we didn't see a need to set up supplies. I can go through your area tomorrow and make sure you guys have all of the necessities, like coffee and tea."

"Great! Maybe one day next week we can go to lunch and get to know each other? I would love to hear any suggestions you have to help me integrate here as well." Excitement coursed through my veins and a smiled was plastered on my face the rest of the day.

"I would love that! This Friday is our monthly dance night. You should consider joining us. Maybe even Paris and her mate can as well?"

Paris had been standing nearby when she heard her name and she came over. "I would love to join you all. But I don't know what plans Venay has. I'll ask him."

I hadn't seen any dancing by any of the V'Zenians yet. "Clarissa, do the aliens know how to dance?"

Paris answered instead. "Actually, Venay does. He surprised me one night before we were mated and put together a very romantic dinner, and we danced. I think that was the night I knew I was falling for him ... hard." She had this dreamy, far-away look in her eyes.

"Some of our guys here can dance. They like to learn, and we do monthly dances and teach them. With a huge influx of women, I bet all of the men turn out this week." She smiled and went back to her filing.

"Paris, how many women will be here by Friday? And what day is today? I have lost all count of days since we left Earth." I tried to think how long we had been here, but I wasn't really sure.

"Um, I think today is Monday. I couldn't tell you what the alien word is, but I heard Venay talking about the day of the week yesterday with Zelan and the translator said it was Sunday."

"Oh, okay, I guess that makes sense. So, I have five days to get a boat load of women transferred here. Hmm, Haver is going to be working overtime I think." I smiled thinking about all the women that were going to be the object of Aysi-aer's flirting. He wasn't going to be upset in the least with all the extra flights.

When we got back to the ship that night, I had a lot of notes from the day. I spent the rest of the evening working out a tentative schedule. First thing on the list was to figure out who was heading to New Hope this week, and then I needed to get the seamstress over here to take measurements for the women.

"Commander, can I schedule a seamstress to come over here tomorrow and get measurements for the first of the women going to New Hope? Oh, and what about the men? Are they going to the settlement as well?" I stood to his side, holding my notepad barely able to keep the excitement from bubbling out.

"Why do you need measurements?" He gruffed.

"Because none of us have anything more than the clothes on our backs. We need more than that. The settlement has a few seamstresses and they make all of their own clothes, so they wanted to get the measurements as soon as they could. They need to schedule the work. Also, I need to poll the women and see who has what skills. We need to match them up with the jobs that need filling first." We hadn't discussed what he wanted me to do first, but I knew this was something that was important.

"Hm, sounds like you already have a full schedule. I need to sit down with you tomorrow and go over what I need from you, but after that go ahead and schedule what you see fit. I would start with the women who have the universal translators first. The men will go, but they are going last. I want the women to get settled in before I release the men. I have a feeling we are going to have some issues with them. They still haven't settled down and accepted their fate. Just the other day, one of them tried to attack one of my warriors." He shook his head.

"Oh, I had hoped they would appreciate going to the colony versus staying in cells. It's too bad because I know that the settlement could use some muscle and some construction workers too. Maybe some of the women can fill those roles." I shrugged my shoulders and went back to working on my schedule.

CHAPTER FIFTEEN

The next day came way too early. "Come on sleepy head, time to get up." I woke up to Commander Venay's face directly in front of mine. It startled me so much I jumped and screamed a bit.

He laughed.

"Really funny, Commander. That is not a nice way to be woken up. What time is it? I feel like I just went to sleep." I rubbed the sleep from my eyes as I sat up.

"It is 6 am local time. We have a lot to do today. So let's get going. First stop is the bridge. You need to meet the crew working there so you can come and go as well as allow you to communicate with the settlement whenever you are on this ship. Your communication device isn't strong enough to reach the settlement, so all comms must go through the bridge, for now. We are working on setting up repeaters so that you can just use your internal comm with anyone no matter where you are."

"Sounds good, but why so early?" I yawned.

"Because you have a very full day if you want to get the seamstresses here and survey the humans for job skills before you move." He took a few steps back and smiled at me. I think he enjoyed waking me up so early.

What a monster, and no coffee here to help me wake up, either.

I sighed deeply. "Yes, of course. Do I have time to get some tea before we leave?"

"Breakfast is ready and waiting for you on the table. We leave in fifteen minutes so get going." He pointed to the kitchen.

He had no clue how long it took women to get ready. I was so happy that he wouldn't be around to wake me up every day. Poor Paris.

True to his word, we left his quarters within fifteen minutes. I wasn't finished with my breakfast, so I just took the toast with me, and ate it while we walked to the bridge.

The Commander stopped me around the corner from the bridge entrance, "Natalie, I need you to be on your best behavior while on the bridge. Most of the warriors here are not mine. They won't be as tolerant of your presence as I am. It might be best if you only come to the bridge with either myself, or Zelan. I would hate to hear you had been treated poorly by one of the bridge officers."

"Won't they respect your word? If you tell them I'm your assistant, doesn't that mean something to them?" I furrowed my brow and hoped that none of them would be rude to me. All sorts of appalling scenarios raced through my brain in just a few seconds.

"To some it will, to others you are just a slave. Even if you are my assistant, you are no better than cattle. I understand both you, and Paris, want to work to improve the status of humans in my world, but this bridge is not a place to experiment. Do you understand?" He looked me straight in the eyes and I felt a little intimidated by the intensity of his look.

"Yes, Sir. I will do my best to stay out of everyone's way

here." It was hard not to cower in his presence when he went all Commander-mode on me.

I followed him into the room and looked around. The bridge was smaller than I expected. It had multiple work stations, and each one was manned by different aliens. A few were pure-bloods, but most were hybrids.

What surprised me the most was the viewscreen. It took up the entire wall in front of the workstations. The captain's chair sat in the middle of the room, like a throne. In front of that was a long workstation where four warriors sat looking at the displays on the tabletops in front of them. If they looked up, they would see a giant screen that had to be bigger than the movie theatre screen back home. Off to the left and the right were more workstations built into the wall.

We walked over to one side, "Natalie, this is my communications officer, Maximillian. Max, this is my new assistant. She will on occasion need to comm the colony, and if she ever sends a message to me from the colony, you are to route it immediately to me. Show her how to send her messages. And be sure to tell your replacement the same thing." I smiled when I saw Max. At least one face on this bridge would be somewhat friendly.

He smiled at me as well, "Natalie, it is good to see you again." He stood up, "Please, take the seat here and I will show you how to send a comm."

The commander looked at me with a stern face, and an arched eyebrow, but said nothing as he walked to his throne chair.

As soon as I finished relaying my message for the seamstresses to come over, the Commander told me to follow him. We went to a room that was off to the side of the bridge.

"This is my office, while on this ship. The only way to enter is via the bridge. If I ever request your presence on the bridge, and I am not there, I will be in here."

"Okay." I wondered what he wanted that had to be said in private.

He must have read my mind, "There will be times when we speak in private because there are factions on this ship who want nothing more than to keep the humans in our cells. Most of those who were serving on this ship are not human friendly, so keep that in mind when making friends. How do you know Max?"

"I met him the other night in the mess hall when we had movie night. He seemed to be fine with me being a human." I wasn't worried about Max, or even his brother. Even though his brother was a flirt.

"I am sure he is, but others are not. Just be careful. It will be better for all humans to move to the settlement as quickly as possible." He then gave me a list of things he wanted done tomorrow. After which, he promptly kicked me off the bridge. Truth be told, I was happy to leave.

While I was getting more comfortable with the Commander, it was still intimidating being on the bridge in front of so many aliens. He was right too, as I walked away, I saw a few of them looking at me with scowls on their faces and even heard one say, "Why did the Commander use a slave as his assistant? Any one of us could have done that job so much better."

I didn't wait around to hear what his companion said, but I was pretty sure it wouldn't have been nice. Those were two guys I would try to avoid at all costs.

Next on my list was heading to the cells to take inventory of job skills. For the most part, I was looking forward to this. However, there were a few people I wasn't looking forward to speaking with. I started with my least favorite person, so that the task could only get better from there.

"Rachelle, have you received your implant yet?" I knew she wasn't scheduled until later, but I wanted to see what she had to say. Maybe things had changed.

"No, I wanted to wait and make sure that it was safe before I signed up." She sniffed. "I'm on the list for next week." She shrugged one shoulder like it was no big deal.

"That's good. I'm here today to take a list of names and job skills. The outpost needs certain positions filled right away. Then they will match the rest up to roles they could use help with. Have you ever sewn anything?" A part of me was glad she was stuck here for another week and wouldn't be able to interfere with Zelan and me.

"Me? No, I'm not a "Susy-homemaker" kind of girl. I am meant for management. My last job was in a bank and I was on the fast track to becoming the youngest bank manager in history." She straightened her shoulders and her haughty look appeared once again. Something she had mastered.

"Huh, well, we don't use money on this planet. Everyone works hard and gets to use the services for free. I'll put down that you are good with counting. That might be a skill set they can use." I wasn't going to put customer service. I could tell she would only provide good customer service to those she wanted something from.

I made my way around the room until lunch time and took a break with Zelan. He came to the holding cells to get me which caused a bit of a stir with Rachelle. "Oh Zelan, is it time for our lunch? I'm looking forward to spending more time with you today." She sidled up as close as she could to the cell bars nearest him and his veins pulsed a bit of orange before he calmed himself. Then his veins went to green.

"Rachelle, for the last time, I am taken. Natalie is my mate. I have no interest in anyone else. Please stop trying to get my attention, it only makes you look bad." He walked past her and straight to me. What he did next caused quite a stir. He took me in his arms and gave me a kiss that caused my knees to go weak. I dropped my pad and pencil when he grabbed me. If he hadn't been holding me so tightly against his body, I might have fallen to the ground.

I heard the catcalls from the guys in the room, and even a few girls were whispering and giggling. Oh well, I guess the cat was out of the bag now. "Hello to you too, Zelan." I said as I tried to get my feet under me again.

"I missed you, Natalie." He whispered in my ear. Then he said a bit louder, "Are you ready for our lunch date?"

I smiled up to him and said, "Yes, let's go." I grabbed his hand after I picked up my fallen notepad and pencil, and we walked out of the room. Men were still whistling and some of the girls said things like, "You go girl!" Another said, "That's the kind of man I want." I tuned them out and focused on Zelan as we headed to lunch.

"Ok mister, what was that display of affection for? I didn't see any warriors in there who were ogling me. So why do that?" I looked up at him with pursed lips, and one eyebrow raised.

"To make sure those women knew I was taken. Sometimes it isn't all about you." He winked at me and my heart thudded loudly.

What do you say to something like that? I didn't have a response, so I kept my eyes forward and thought about what he said. Sometimes, I could be a bit egocentric. The world didn't revolve around me, and I knew this. However, it was always good to get a reminder.

Zelan had to have had more than one other admirer. I could only imagine how rotten it was for him to fend off women if they were anything like Rachelle. I only hoped there weren't any alluring women who wanted Zelan.

We went to his room where he had laid out sandwiches. It was an impressive spread. The ham and swiss looked wonderful, so I chose that. It was fairly quiet, and I started to get nervous. Even though I enjoyed being alone with him, I didn't want anything to happen between us yet. His nearness affected me more than I wanted to admit and my breathing still hadn't gone back to normal after that kiss.

"Zelan, do you really think it's safe for us to live here?" I know, it was a major change in topic, but it was something that had been on my mind since the attack the other day.

"Of course, it is. We will make it even safer with all the upgrades. The Commander mentioned the other day that we are in the process of obtaining a new satellite, remember?"

"Yes, but isn't it like five months away from here?" I put my sandwich down and looked up at Zelan with furrowed brows. Waiting five months for the protection the new satellite would provide was worth it, but it wouldn't do us any good until it actually arrived, which was five months away. So why did he think it would make a difference now?

"Actually, it is less than a month away. There is another settlement that makes the satellites. This one we have coming was intended for another planet, but since we have these issues now, the President re-routed it to us as soon as he heard about the attack." He took a bite of his sandwich.

Then he continued, "This satellite will allow us to scan the planet for technology and advanced life-forms. We are also worried about finding any other ships that the bugs may have sent here. I think our first concern is finding that crashed ship of theirs and destroying it. Then, we need to find any mutant cockroaches that survived, or were hatched here, and destroy them."

"Will the satellite do anything else for us?" I hoped it had some defensive capabilities as well.

"It does help with detecting ships that enter this solar system. We will have a better view of anyone who tries to come here again. There is also a communication node inside that will help us to communicate from anywhere on this planet using our universal translators." He paused before continuing and sighed.

"They will, of course have to be synced to the satellite's software. However, you should know, that it will also be able to track our movements. It isn't so much of a tracking tool, as a communication tool. I know you don't want to be tracked, but it could be helpful in finding you if you ever get lost, or something happens to you. Or anyone for that matter." He cupped my cheek and rubbed his thumb across my cheekbone, which sent chills down my entire body.

I heaved a heavy sigh. "I understand why you think that is important. Us humans are going to have trouble with being tracked, it's a bit too *1984* for us."

"1984? Isn't that a year from your planet's history? What does that have to do with this conversation?" He scratched his chin after taking a bite of his sandwich.

"That was a book written a long time ago by an author who predicted that our governments would take control of our lives and watch our every move. Since then, we have seen a lot of that happening. Many of our personal freedoms have been violated because of the watchful eyes of our governments. Sometimes it really is for the betterment of all people, but sometimes it is just the government flexing its muscle." I took a small bite of my sandwich.

"There was a scandal not long ago about the government actively reading our emails, and listening to our cell phone calls. Now granted, if we had nothing to hide, then it shouldn't have mattered. But, some of those messages were very personal. People don't like it when strangers listen to their intimate communications." I wiped my mouth and took a drink of water.

"The idea of that listening program was a good one, but it turned out to be a huge nightmare for our government and her allies. We want our anonymity. The ability to move about and communicate without someone watching us has always been very important. We call it "Big Brother." You know, the guy who is always looking over your shoulder at everything you're doing? As a people, we don't like it."

"I see. We have a lot of freedom, but no one actively listens to our communications or reads our messages.

Although, in theory, it is possible that someone could do it. We just don't do that. The only people who are ever tracked are slaves who run away." He looked down at his plate.

"Um, well. Why don't we turn our conversation to something a bit lighter? What time are we leaving tonight? I still have more people to interview." I put my sandwich down as I had lost my appetite.

"We will be on the 1900 flight back to the colony. I hope that helps you to schedule the rest of your afternoon?" He quirked his lips and I could feel the tension leaving us both as we switched the topic.

"Yes. Zelan that will work fine for my schedule. I hope I can spend the majority of my day tomorrow in the office working on setting it all up and getting used to the computers you use. I like the idea of them, but they are very different. So futuristic compared to what I'm used to." Everything was moving so fast and work was already piling up. I had so much to do I felt like I needed an assistant of my own. Once I had a chance to settle in, I was sure I'd feel more capable and organized. Or at least, I hoped I did.

"Don't worry, I will spend the morning with you and help you get up to speed. I am confident that you will catch on quickly." He took my hand and pulled it to his lips and kissed the back of it. When he pulsed purple, I relaxed and enjoyed the rest of our meal.

The next few days flew by. I picked up on the computer quickly, just like Zelan said I would. They were really cool too! You could choose between reading on the tablet, or bringing up the 3D display. Since I loved the idea of using a new interface, I always chose the 3D display, except for when I was around others. Then I used the tablet for privacy. It was light weight and compact and easy to carry around. It reminded me of my iPad Pro I had back home.

There was a book bag that held the tablet and a few other supplies in it perfectly. I used that to carry it around whenever I wasn't in the office. The Commander expected me to have it on me at all times, so I never went anywhere without it.

My relationship with Zelan was moving along very smoothly. He even brought me a flower yesterday morning when he came into the office. It was a hibiscus, just like the one someone left me after my procedure last week.

As much as I enjoyed his attentions, I was still a bit leery. One day I was fine with being his mate. The next day all of the issues come to mind, and I found myself struggling with it again. That just meant I wasn't ready. Thankfully, everyone had stopped pressuring me to accept him since we moved here.

CHAPTER SIXTEEN

About a week after I moved to the settlement, Haver discovered what looked like wreckage from a ship in one of his reconnaissance missions. I heard it through the grapevine. No one could keep a secret here. Well, except for me. I was able to keep secrets from getting out when the Commander told me something in the strictest of confidence. But this news was spreading like wildfire all over the colony.

I comm'd Zelan the second I walked away from the person who told me. "Zelan, is it true? Did you guys find the insectoid crashed ship?"

"Wow, that didn't take long. Who told you? Clarissa?"

"No, it was Janice. I went to pick up some new shoes, and she was telling someone else in the clothing warehouse. I just left there."

"How did she hear it?"

"No clue. So it's true?" I couldn't believe it. The fear of another attack had been getting to me at times. With this new information, we could eradicate the bugs and I could finally sleep well. I hadn't told anyone, but one of the reasons I chose a bunk in the first bunkhouse I was shown was because I wanted to be with others in case of an attack. I figured there was safety in numbers and all that. Plus, these ladies all had more knowledge and experience on this planet than I did, and they would have known exactly what to do in a crisis.

"Yes, Haver isn't even back yet from the scouting mission. We are getting together tonight to plan an attack for first light tomorrow. I am hoping to use the sun as part of our attack."

"So, that means no date tonight?" We had been out every night since we moved here. If I was honest with myself, I would agree to marry him, but I was too stubborn to give in so soon.

"I am sorry, but I won't be able to see you tonight. Can we reschedule for tomorrow night? After we are finished, I will have to debrief everyone, but then I will be free for dinner, at least. Can we make plans?"

He sounded so sad. I wished there was something I could do for him, but this was his job and he had to do it. "Are your veins pulsing blue right now?"

He chuckled. "How did you know?"

"Because, I'm in tune with you and your emotions. I feel the same way. As much as I want to see you tonight, I know your job is very important, and this discovery is too big to put off. You have to attack right away. I'll be here waiting for your safe return." If I could have, my veins would have been pulsing blue in time with his, I just knew it. We had gotten very close very quickly. It scared me at times and at other times I felt loved and wanted. And dare I say … needed. Emotions Ben never instilled in me.

I really needed to stop comparing Zelan to Ben. There was no comparison, Zelan was more of a man than Ben was, and Zelan's an alien! How sad was that?

That night Paris came to the colony, and she was going to spend the night. The Commander thought this mission was too important to stay away from. Even though he intended to let Zelan lead the planning and attack, he was going to be on the team.

"Paris, do you want pancakes for dinner? You look sad. Maybe they will cheer you up like they do for me." She was slowly walking with me to her apartment.

They had set up a place here so that whenever either of them came over they had a place that was theirs. She hoped to see her husband, but knew that he would be out late, so she asked me to dinner.

"Sorry, I'm not in the best of moods tonight. Venay has been working so hard that I have hardly seen him. Tonight was supposed to be a date night. Maybe tomorrow night we can stay here and have a special night on the town." She shook her head and sighed.

"Wow, you have it bad, don't you?" I chuckled as I steered her away from the apartment and toward the pancake house.

"Huh? Oh, yeah, I guess so. It's just that he promised me a week away in the mountains once we got settled into the new ship. He hasn't had the time to take off, and I really want that alone time. Did you know they have a spa, of sorts, up in the mountains here?" Her pain was evident in the way her eyes were downcast and the sadness coming through her voice.

"Really? That sounds quite relaxing. Maybe after they destroy the ship you two can take off. It will make it much safer for you to go away. Right now, it isn't safe on this planet to be anywhere, especially if it is just the two of you."

"I know. I guess I'm being a bit melodramatic. Pancakes for dinner sounds decadent. Let's do it." She seemed a bit more upbeat as we made our way to the restaurant.

Once we were settled at a corner booth, and had received our order, the first words out of Paris' mouth were, "Oh my word! You were right about these. I know where I am going whenever I need a little taste of home."

"I told you they were great!" We spent a couple of hours there chatting with everyone.

The news about the upcoming mission was all anyone could talk about. It was well past closing time when we left the place. They normally closed much earlier, but with so many who wanted to stay and discuss the impending attack tomorrow, the manager kept it open.

On this planet they had a 25 hour day, and they used military time, which meant it was past 2400 when we left for home.

The extra hour was interesting. We still slept about seven hours a night, but with an extra hour in the day, people seemed to be a bit more productive. School for the kids ended on a normal time. With the extra hour they were able to get homework done and have time to play with their friends.

Workers split the time. A typical work day here had an extra thirty minutes. Since no one walked more than thirty minutes to work, they all had a well-rounded day. More time was spent with family and friends.

Once I was back in my bunk I couldn't sleep. All I could think about was Zelan and his mission. In order to keep sane, I thought about plans for the next week. During the week I had been here, I discovered some more fun things to do. Once the mission was over, I was going to make reservations for Zelan and me to play mini-golf one night next week. He didn't know it yet, but he was going to get a typical Earth date soon.

There was a BBQ planned and a dance the following week that I hoped to be able to attend as well. It really was the best of both worlds here. My aim was to get Zelan to fall in love with the colony and decide to stay here with me. I fell asleep planning how I was going to arrange it.

The next day I woke up early. My body knew where it needed to be, no sleeping in for me. it was desperate to be somewhere I could get up to date information.

Since I was the Commander's assistant, I was allowed entry into the command center for the mission.

When I walked into the command center, I suddenly stopped from the shock of who I saw in the room and had to remember to not let my emotions show on my face. "Good morning, Captain. I'm surprised to see you here and not on the mission with the rest of the warriors." Captain Mypo seemed like a very able captain so I was stunned she wasn't chosen to go on this mission.

"It was deemed best for someone of my rank to stay here and protect the settlement in case of any issues. While I would have preferred to go on this mission, I understand how dangerous it is to leave my colony unprotected." She went back to monitoring the comm channel as the ship approached the site. "Take a seat, Natalie, and watch how effective our warriors are at destroying the enemy."

A chill went down my spine as she spoke. Adrenaline coursed through my veins as I watched the screen on the wall. Some of the warriors wore helmet cams. I was going to be able to watch them as they attacked the ship. No one told me they had this type of equipment. Although, I shouldn't have been surprised, even Earth forces had them.

Haver sent back images to us of the crashed ship as he flew near the site. It was smaller than our ship and it had a saucer shape to it. If I didn't know any better, I would swear that it was the same type of craft that crashed in Roswell, New Mexico back in the 1940's.

"Son of a biscuit eater!"I had programmed my translator

to use some funnier Earth slang when a V'Zenian cussed in their language. I was tired of hearing all the rotten language that came from the mouths of the warriors now that I had my universal translator. "They have a ship that is half Zateelian and half Q'Tuelien in design! Why weren't we told that they had broken our treaty and gave their technology to our enemy?" Commander Croso exclaimed.

Commander Croso stood up and paced back and forth after slamming his hand onto the console in front of him. "Why is there even a question as to *if* we will go to war with those cockroaches? It should be a done deal! The only question should be if we go to war with the QT's as well." He crossed his arms and tapped his left foot.

"Commander, I don't know if the war council has seen images of the Zateelian's ship. Maybe we need to send these to the President directly?" The Captain stood up and was doing something on her console. If I had to guess, I would say she was copying the images to send to their President.

"I saw the images from the battle in space. It wasn't obvious that the Zateelians had so much of the QT's armament. That laser cannon over there, next to the cluster of banyan trees, that is their latest piece of equipment. There is no way the Zateelians could have come up with that design on their own. It was given to them by the QT's." Commander Croso pounded his hand on the wall next to the screen. It shivered a little bit as the wall moved with the force of his punch.

The Captain pointed out more technology that belonged to the QT's.

"Captain, how do you know so much about their technology?" I asked.

She cleared her throat. "We may or may not have intercepted an intel packet of theirs." She kept her eyes on the screen and didn't look my way at all.

Interesting, so the QT's were allies on paper only. Made

sense. I supposed Earth Allies spied on each other as well, so it wasn't too strange that aliens did the same thing.

The ship landed and all eyes went to the screens while the chatter stopped instantly. It was like someone turned the volume off on a TV. One minute there was noise all over the room, the next, it was completely devoid of sound.

The Commander pushed a button on the console in front of him, and we could hear the communication from the mission team.

I sat up straighter and focused on the screen and cleared my mind of all thoughts. This was not the time to think about work or anything else. Now was the time to focus on Zelan. He took point as they walked out of the ship. One of the cameras was right behind him. He pushed the comm on his neck. "Command, this is Alpha One Leader, do you copy?"

Commander Croso replied, "This is Command. You have a go."

They left the safety of the ship and moved toward the debris. On different screens I could see the various vegetation mixed with parts of the crashed ship. The animals must not have sensed our guys because I could still hear birds chirping and a few roars from what must have been a large cat, maybe a lion?

Zelan motioned, and his team split up into two groups. I watched only the screen with Zelan. My heart was racing, and I hoped he would be alright.

I had noticed that Venay took a squad and went in another direction, but I was more interested in following what Zelan was up to so I ignored the images from Venay's team.

Zelan held up his hand in a fist, and everyone stopped. I could see his head moving in different directions, and then he went to the left. A camera followed him, so I assumed the rest of his squad did as well. After a few minutes I could see more debris from the ship, which included another one of those laser cannons that the Commander pointed out earlier.

The camera panned down for a good look at the cannon. Then it panned back up and followed Zelan. Within ten minutes they had a visual on the ship. He put up his fist again and the camera stopped its forward momentum. It panned to the left and the right slowly so we could get a good look at everything.

There were multiple mutant cockroaches outside the ship under a camouflage tarp. The green and brown tarps had been placed in various spots along the side of the ship. This must have been one of the ways they kept their location a secret for so long. Haver and Aysiaer did a great job with their recon if they were able to locate the ship with it's disguise.

There must have been at least twelve bugs outside standing guard.

I heard another roar, and the guards turned toward their ship but then looked back out to the jungle.

I watched as Zelan pointed two fingers to the left and two to the right. Then he used three fingers to point forward. The camera was still behind Zelan, thankfully, as they slowly moved forward.

My breath caught in my throat as I watched in horror.

All at once, the mutant bugs looked right at the camera. They must have heard or sensed our warriors. I heard a screeching sound, and then the bugs ran toward my man. He pointed his phaser gun at the closest bug and fired. It was a direct hit to its face. The thing fell down but there was another directly behind it.

Zelan and the others, continued to fire at the bugs, who had guns as well and pointed them at our group. They fired at the camera, and it looked like a laser had been shot right at me. I couldn't help but jump in my seat.

The cameraman dove to the left in time to miss being hit.

I heard him grunt, so he might have been grazed along the arm or shoulder. He got up quickly and panned around looking for the bug that shot him, but it was already down.

The cameraman continued to fire at the enemy as he made his way to Zelan's side. They were both firing at the heads of the insectoids closest to them. The enemy continued to fire at them while they scurried closer, and closer. Both Zelan and the camera took cover behind the nearest tree and then took turns firing from the sides of the trunk. Laser fire was all over the screen. This fight looked like something out of a sci-fi movie instead of my life.

Zelan continued to fire at the insectoids as the cameraman climbed up the tree. He began to shoot into the mob of bugs once he got into position directly above where Zelan had been standing.

More enemies came flooding out of the ship, too many to count. It looked like hundreds of them. They were surrounding our guys … my Zelan.

My heart felt like it would explode with the fear and dread of what I could see taking place on the screen.

I had no idea how Zelan was going to get out of this, but he had to. He had to come home to me. There were too many of them to fight off.

Retreat, retreat. I pleaded mentally. I didn't want anyone to think I was a coward, but I was. I wasn't a warrior. All I wanted was for Zelan to come back to me safe and sound. I knew they had to eradicate the Zateelians, I knew it. But that didn't mean I wanted Zelan leading the charge.

My hand went to my heart and I massaged the space above the organ that was about ready to break.

Zelan yelled via his comm, "NOW!"

I watched in horror as the screen grew bright, and the image coming from the camera flew backwards. It flicked out, and all was black on the screen.

"NO!" I jumped up and started toward the screen. "Get

that image back. We have to know what's going on!" I yelled as cold sweat dripped from my head.

I grabbed my head and yelled, "NO, they can't be gone!" I looked around furiously at the other screens, but they had all gone blank as well. "What happened? Was there an explosion?"

The Captain looked at me, and my body chilled from the sadness I saw in her eyes. "Yes, it was a failsafe, in case they were to be overrun. Captain Zelan ordered the ship to be targeted and fired upon with a missile from our transport shuttle. There was no way any of our warriors were going to allow themselves to be used as hosts for the enemy's hatchlings. Every one of them agreed to this before going on the mission. This was why you were not allowed in that briefing. I am sorry, Natalie, but it appears..."

A static noise interrupted the Captain. "..his ... lan ... me?" I could only make out a few syllables, but it sounded like someone survived the attack.

"This is Commander Croso. Who is this? Identify yourself!"

The voice was weak, but the static had dissipated. "Commander, this is Captain Zelan. The ship is destroyed. Most of the enemy are dead, but I see a few slowly moving about. Are the cameras still working? I don't see my team."

I opened my mouth to say something, but nothing came out. Tears were streaming down my cheeks as I stared at the screens, willing them to work again.

"Captain, none of the cameras are working. Can you make it back to the ship? Can all of your warriors make it back?" the Commander asked.

"I will see who can make it back without help. Don't let the transport leave without us."

"Should I send one of our pilots out to help you? "

"Negative, we will carry our wounded and dead back ourselves. Just have the ship ready to take off and ready another missile to send into the area again as we leave, just to make sure we got them all."

"Yes Captain, I will inform Haver right away." The Commander comm'd for Haver, "Lieutenant Haver, do you read?"

"This is Haver. Did anyone survive?" He sounded tentative, as though he had been holding his breath waiting for the bad news.

"Yes, they are making their way back to you now. Be prepared to take off right away and shoot another missile into the enemy camp as you do."

"Yes, Sir. Haver out."

All I could do at this point was wait for them to get to the ship and take off. Once we got confirmation that they were up I would feel a whole lot better. I cleared the tears off my face and looked at the other people in the room. Even a few of them had tears streaming down their face. To hear that some survived was a miracle.

I paced as I waited for any information to come our way. I was so very grateful that Zelan had survived, but I wondered about the rest. Who made it? Who didn't?

It was a long thirty minutes until we received the message that they had made it back to the shuttle. I practically dropped with relief when I heard Haver telling command that everyone was onboard.

My breath hitched and I thought I had caught a glimpse of Zelan from the ship's exterior camera, but all of the warriors were so dirty and the alien I thought was my man had another alien over his shoulder, so the view wasn't very good.

We watched the exterior cameras from Haver's ship as the missile hit its target. Once the area on the camera blew up, not a single person in the room –alien or otherwise– were sitting. We all jumped up and shouted for joy! The tears were gone, and everyone was smiling and yelling.

I backed up into the wall behind me and breathed a sigh of relief as I waited for Zelan to get back.

The Captain came over to me, "Well, I guess now that you have seen how brave our new Captain is, will you be changing your mind about him?" She arched her eyebrows and walked away before I could comment.

What would I say to him? When I thought he was dead, I realized I wanted him, needed him. But I did not want to be on a battle cruiser in the middle of a war. The two battles I had witnessed were enough to tell me that I couldn't handle it. I would most likely end up with a heart attack. My heart was still beating heavily in my chest. I put my hands to my heart and felt the muscle beating out its complaint.

Then my head shot up as I realized I hadn't heard anything about Commander Venay. "Commander Croso, any word on Commander Venay? Did he make it?" I walked over to where the Commander and Captain were looking at images on their desktop screens.

"Yes, he had taken another squad, and they were further out from the enemy ship than your Captain was. He has some injuries, but no one was seriously hurt. Zelan's team took the brunt of the explosion. They all have some injuries, and two of his warriors are dead. They will be here within the next ten minutes if you want to go and wait for them in the hangar.

"Thank you, Commander. Yes. I'll go wait for them there. Has anyone told Paris yet?"

"No, I assumed Venay would comm her," the Captain replied.

I smiled and ran toward the hanger bay. On the way I comm'd Paris, and she had just spoken to Commander Venay. He was just fine. She was on her way to meet me.

When they landed Paris and I were both there waiting for our men. I was bouncing on my feet by the time Zelan walked out. He didn't look good. My warrior was covered in soot, blood, leaves, and who knew what else. But I didn't care.

I ran into his arms and almost knocked him to the ground with my enthusiasm. I kissed him, not caring that his lips were dirty. He wrapped his arms around me and kissed me back. I could taste the acidic ash that was on his lips and thought nothing in the world tasted better.

"Zelan, I'm so glad you're okay!" I exclaimed as I pulled back from him. "What happened? Why were there so many bugs there? I saw on the monitors in the control room. How could they have had so many bodies? That makes no sense, not after we killed at least a thousand of them last week."

"Natalie, my love. I am so glad to see you! I will answer your questions later. First, I need a shower, and then I have to take care of my men. Will you go back to my apartment and wait for me?" He took my hands in his and kissed them.

"Yes, of course I will wait for you there. Hurry up." I looked over at Paris and Commander Venay. "Commander, it is good to see you are alright as well. I'm sorry for the losses, but very glad so many of you made it back safely."

He put his arm around Paris. "Thank you, Natalie. I will see you first thing tomorrow in the office. Zelan, you got the debrief?"

"Yes, Sir. I have told the men to shower than meet me in the control room, and we will debrief tonight before going home." Zelan must have been in pain, he wasn't standing as erect as he normally did when addressing the Commander. In fact, he was a bit hunched over and when I looked in his eyes, I saw it. He was holding it together for the Commander, and maybe even me, but he was in a lot of pain.

"Good, get a good night's sleep. You did great today. I am honored to call you one of my best warriors. It was very brave of you to order the missile strike before you got out of the line of fire." The Commander nodded to Zelan and walked away. Paris waved to me as they left.

"I can't believe you did that. How could you take a chance like that? You almost got blown up with those bugs. I never would have forgiven you if you had." I hugged him close to me.

He sighed and rubbed my back, then whispered in my ear, "It is good to see you care so much." He kissed my ear, and then slowly kissed his way down my neck but stopped when he got to my shirt collar and sighed. "I will see you in a few hours." He kissed my cheek quickly and walked away.

"Oh, I'm in trouble." I whispered to myself. That man was a heart attack waiting to happen. I rubbed the pain in my chest as I turned and walked to his apartment. Once I was outside, I noticed how dirty I was and turned toward my barracks so I could shower and put on clean clothes while I waited for him to get done.

CHAPTER SEVENTEEN

I was so exhausted from the stress and the adrenaline rush that I fell asleep in Zelan's chair. He picked me up and brought me to his bed when he came in. "Hey, sorry I fell asleep. Is everyone going to be okay?"

"Yes, other than the two warriors I lost today, everyone else is fine. A few needed attention from the doctor, but nothing too serious." He kissed my forehead after he laid down next to me. "I really need you right now. Would you mind sleeping here with me tonight? I promise I will behave." His smile wasn't his usual one, and he pulsed blue.

His emotions filled me, and I wasn't sure If I was feeling sad on my own or if he was affecting me. It was so confusing. All I knew was that I needed him.

"Of course, I could use your arms around me right about now." I leaned up and gave him a quick kiss on the lips before turning so that we were spooning. He put one arm under my neck and the other was resting comfortably around my torso. It felt right to be in his arms like this. I wasn't going to overthink it. We both needed the comfort after what happened today, and I had zero desire to do anything more than sleep in his arms. From the looks of him, I doubted he wanted anything more either.

"Zelan, what happened? How did they have so many mutants? Do that many travel in their ships?" I didn't see them all, but I did overhear one of the warriors counting on the screens. He said it had to be over one hundred and fifty bugs that he could see, and who knew how many more were in the ship.

"I didn't see it, but Commander Venay saw a pile of Z'Girguan's. They are indigenous to this planet and look similar to your lions. It is believed that the Zateelians are using those animals to reproduce." He nuzzled my neck before continuing.

"We knew they could use other warm-blooded animals as hosts but did not realize that they had already discovered the Z'Girguan's were compatible. I was hoping that none of the animals here would be so well-matched. Not all will be." He kissed my forehead, and then he laid back down. After a few minutes I could hear him start to breathe a bit heavier. He must have been utterly exhausted.

I looked back over my shoulder and his were closed. It didn't take me long to fall asleep either.

The next morning, he woke me up with a kiss to my neck. I smiled as the remnants of a wonderful dream went through my mind. We had married, and I was pregnant with our third child. What a dream to wake up remembering. My body was screaming for me to accept my fate and mate with this wonderful, alien man. But my mind was telling me not yet.

I turned around so that I was facing him. "Good morning. How did you sleep?"

"It was strange. I had a dream where we were mated, and you were pregnant with our third child. I want that vision to come true, Natalie." He caressed my face with one hand and kissed the tip of my nose. "No pressure, but if I agreed to stay here, would you become my mate?" The earnestness in his eyes pierced my heart and I was lost.

Could it be true? Were we supposed to be together? After yesterday and almost losing him, I knew I couldn't let him go. Plus, this shared dream made me believe that he really was my true mate.

How was it that we shared a dream? Was it one of those fated mates things? Did it happen because he held me all night long? Surely it wasn't coincidence. While I believed in coincidence, this was too much.

I leaned in and kissed him good and hard, not caring about morning breath. He rolled me onto my back and leaned his body over the top of mine. He put most of his weight on one of his arms and let his other hand roam over my body. I opened my lips to accept him, and he bit my lower lip before giving me what I wanted.

My hands were roaming over his shirtless back. I could feel the ripples in his muscles and it turned me on even more. He pulled back, breathing heavily. "Does that mean, *yes?*"

I took a moment to get a good, deep breath. "Yes, if you can get assigned here, I will marry you as soon as possible." He kissed me again, and it was at least an hour before we got out of bed.

That afternoon when we had lunch, Zelan told me that the Commander granted his request to stay. "I think that due to the Zateelian issue, it will take longer than the next four months to eradicate the bugs. This settlement is going to need fully trained warriors to stay here for some time to come."

"I wonder if Earth's pesticides would work on the tiny, mutant cockroaches. Next time someone goes there, they should pick up a bunch of cockroach spray. We could regularly spray the area surrounding the settlement if it works. I doubt it would work on the grown ones, but maybe on the newly hatched it would?" It was a stretch, but totally worth trying.

"Hmm. Maybe when the Commander's new ship arrives, he can find a way to go to Earth before heading off to war."

That just might work for Paris' plan too. Maybe she could start working on a way to get volunteers to come out here so that the V'Zenians could stop abducting humans.

"So, this means we can really get married? Can we have Commander Venay perform the ceremony for us? I know that Croso is in charge here, but since we know Venay so much better, I would like for him to do it. What do you think?"

He smiled. "I take it this means you have given it more thought since this morning in bed?"

My cheeks heated and I looked down at my plate and whispered, "I want to continue what we started this morning, but not until we are married. I saved myself for my future husband all these years and I want to wait until our official mating before we go further. Are you okay with that?" This topic made me nervous. I wanted more with Zelan, but I wanted to wait for our wedding night even more.

Ben was fine waiting, but now I knew it was because he never cared much for me. Zelan, on the other hand, was very obvious with his feelings for me. It took him over an hour to turn his red pulsing veins back to purple this morning.

He reached out for my hand. "Natalie, I told you I would wait, and I meant it. But that doesn't mean that I want to put off our ceremony now that you have agreed. How about we see if Commander Venay can perform our ceremony some-time this week?"

My heart started beating very quickly with anticipation. "Yes, as soon as possible would be great. Now that you are permanently assigned here, there's nothing to stop us." I took a deep breath and felt my eyes tear up a bit.

This was what I wanted. That dream was shared between the both of us for a reason. I was meant for this life and didn't want to put it off any longer.

There were still issues I needed to work through, but Zelan was not going to be involved in the slave trade. Maybe I could even use my position here to help advance this settlement, and maybe even one day we could show the President how much humans can give back when we are free and not burdened with the yoke of slavery.

I couldn't keep the smile off my face as I leaned in for a kiss and started to plan my wedding. Paris was going to be so excited! I hoped she would be my maid of honor.

Once we have dealt with this cockroach infestation, we could re-focus on ways to stop slavery. Hopefully one day soon, we could even open up discussions with the leaders of Earth and get some trading set up between the two species. There were so many positive options moving forward. I had a permanent smile the rest of the day.

EPILOGUE

It only took us two days to put together our mating ceremony. The entire settlement was very excited about it. Some thought it was the perfect way to try and move forward from our losses.

"Paris, I'm so nervous! Was it like this for you?" She had to be nervous on her mating day, right?

Paris chuckled and hugged me, but not too tight as I was wearing my wedding dress. The seamstresses here worked overtime creating a beautiful, white gown for me. "Yes, I was nervous, and also so excited that I put my nerves aside in order to enjoy the day."

"That's a good idea. I'll try that. Zelan said we can go away for a couple of days once the bugs are destroyed. I'm bummed that we don't get a proper honeymoon right now. I guess that's how you feel too?" Butterflies were zooming all around my stomach and my entire body tingled with anticipation.

"Yes, but I know that when we do go away, it will be perfect. I wouldn't want to leave right now, not when there are so many unknowns on this planet. It would be even worse if Venay was called back as soon as we got there. I'll wait." She shrugged her shoulders as she walked around me checking my dress and hair.

"Paris, thank you for being my maid of honor. No one else could have taken on this role." I took her hands in mine and did my best to hold back the tears threatening to form.

"Natalie, I'm honored to be chosen as your maid of honor. I think Venay is also honored to be the one who performs your ceremony. Technically, it should be Commander Croso, since he is the colony leader. But I think he understands. He might even enjoy just sitting there and watching for a change." She smoothed a few strands of hair away from my face. "Now, no tears. Otherwise you'll mess up your perfect make-up."

We both giggled and I blinked back the tears that were threating to spill.

I never thought I'd marry a man I loved. I knew life wouldn't be perfect but marrying someone I had real feelings for who also loved me was a dream come true.

"I think you're perfect. Are you ready?" She walked over and picked up my bouquet.

"Yes, I am. Clarissa sure was sweet to put this hibiscus bouquet together for me, wasn't she?" I smelled the beautiful flowers in my hand and thought back to a family trip to Hawaii. For one brief moment, I was sad that my parents couldn't be here for this. But I wasn't going to let it ruin my day.

I thought back to Zelan and all the wonderful things he had done for me and I just knew ... it was going to be a perfect day, and a perfect marriage.

Paris led me to the door that would open up to my wonderful new beginning.

**Keep reading for a sneak peek at Worlds Entwined!

Book 3, Worlds Entwined is now available!

You can also keep reading to get a snippet of the book!

And if you enjoy Christmas books with a taste of urban fantasy, then check out my Miss Clause series. The Mr. Claus series is coming Christmas 2021. All books with my name on them are PG-13 or PG.

If you want to stay up to date with my writing and what's coming next, follow me on one, or all, of the sites below!

Facebook: https://www.facebook.com/JLHendricksAuthor/

Twitter: https://twitter.com/TinkFan25

Follow me on BookBub if you just want new release notices: https://www.bookbub.com/authors/j-l-hendricks

And if you want to join my newsletter, I'll send you a free book! I have a prequel novella, Worlds Revealed, in the Worlds Away series that is only available to newsletter subscribers. It tells the true story of Roswell and how the V'Zenians saved us.

If you want to make sure you hear about the latest and greatest, or just get your copy of Worlds Revealed, sign up for my newsletter at: https://jlhendricksauthor.com/

newsletter/ I will only send out a few e-mails a month. I hate spam and lots of e-mails from others, so why would I do that to you? I won't. And I will never sell your address either. I will however, do cover reveals, snippets of new books and giveaways or promos in the newsletter, some of which will only be available to newsletter subscribers.

ACKNOWLEDGMENTS

My beta readers are awesome!!! I have two who returned and added a few new ones too. Thank you so much to Leo Roars, Dawnya Goode, Kathy Knuckles, and Angela Weiner. You ladies did a great job catching anything that made it past all of the edits and re-writes! This is a much cleaner manuscript because of your efforts!

A special shout out to my peeps in the 20BooksTo50K group! You all rock!!! Thank you all so much for your help and support!

I have truly come a long way since I first published back in 2016, and I have Michael Anderle to thank for it all. There are also a ton of indie authors who have helped me along the way. But it was Michael who got me started in this business of storytelling. I always had stories running through my mind, but I hadn't tried to put them down on paper in a very long time. Thank you, Michael, for always believing in me and supporting me, you ROCK!

I have had such a blast writing this series so far! It started out as a fantasy about me getting abducted. Of course, it was after I read my first clean Sci-fi romance book. In my vision, I was Paris. Worlds Collide is an extension of that fantasy. Worlds Entwined is a culmination of that dream!

There was also a part of Natalie's past that is actually from my own past. When in college I did a study abroad to Estonia for a semester and I experienced culture shock. I'm not normally someone who gets depressed, but there are things that can trigger it. Culture shock is very common when you are in a totally new environment for a long period of time. I met a missionary who took me under her wing. She and her family were so wonderful to me. She really did make pancakes and maple syrup from scratch because at the time, no stores in Tartu, Estonia sold syrup. They also didn't sell Bisquick, which is what I normally use when making pancakes at home. She didn't put chocolate chips in them like my Aunt has done my entire life, but the Missionary's pancakes were fantastic. One night we also watched When Harry Met Sally. At the time, it was one of my favorite movies and she had the VHS. Yes, this was back before DVD was popular LOL. I'm old.

I can't wait to hear what you have to say about this book! I read all the reviews on the eBook retailer sites. I have been so happy with what I have read! Even the low starred reviews are good to read. They show me where I need to improve. An editor and other authors can help me a lot, but it is the reader's opinions that are the most important. So, keep providing me with your reviews!

Currently, there are two short stories in this world. One is the story of a young widow named, Maddie. Worlds Explode is out now if you want to read her story! It's pretty exciting and fun. The other is Worlds Revealed and tells the true story of Roswell from Venay's grandfather's perspective! Currently only available to those who join my newsletter.

And of course, Worlds Entwined is now available!

CONNECTING WITH ME

If you want to make sure you hear about the latest and great-est, as well as get a free book, sign up for my newsletter at: http://jlhendricksauthor.com/newsletter/ I will only send out a few e-mails a month. I hate spam and lots of e-mails from others, so why would I do that to you? I won't. And I will never sell your address either. I will however, do cover reveals, snippets of new books and giveaways or promos in the newsletter, some of which will only be available to news-letter subscribers.

The rest of my social media addresses are:

Facebook: https://www.facebook.com/JLHendricksAuthor/
Twitter: https://twitter.com/TinkFan25

Follow me on BookBub if you just want new release notices: https://www.bookbub.com/authors/j-l-hendricks

Slave or volunteer? What will the V'Zenian's choose?

With war on the horizon with the Zateelians, Paris and Venay are ordered back to Earth to abduct 2,000 factory workers, along with more women to be used as mates. Will Paris be able to change the minds of Central Command in time? Or will she be forced along with Venay to continue abducting humans instead of recruiting volunteers?

When Paris comes up with an exciting plan which will also include an Interstellar Dating Agency, will Venay talk his leaders into listening to his human mate? Or will he shut up and follow orders?

Eereen – Venay's Second in Command. His future mate is being feisty and refuses to mate with him. If she doesn't change her mind, he could lose her forever.

Come and join the exciting trip back to Earth for the labor force needed to assist with the war effort against the Zateelians! If you have enjoyed the first two books in this series, then you will absolutely fall in love with Worlds Entwined! This is a pg-13 alien abduction adventure full of alien battles with mutant cockroaches, and feisty Earth girls.

PROLOGUE

I met her three months ago and I just knew, I knew she was the one. She doesn't believe it. She thinks that I am manipulating her emotions. There are times where she might feel intense desire for me based on what I am feeling at the moment, but overall, her emotions are hers. I do not understand why Sarah does not recognize her own feelings for me.

Not one couple has taken this long to mate. She even refuses to see me more than twice a week.

I received a message from Command yesterday, offering me my own ship. Now that I have been Captain for a year, I qualify to captain my own starship. If I leave, I am not allowed to take Sarah with me unless she agrees to be my mate. There is no way I can leave her.

Maybe I should tell her? Would she agree to mate with me if she knew I was to have command of a starship and leave this planet? Probably not.

Venay has new orders, the kind that will keep me here or at least close by for a while. I could use the time to convince Sarah she really is in love with me, if she would just give me the chance.

I thought for sure she would have agreed to be my mate after the attack at Zeronzen Lake almost three months ago. Right after that incident, multiple couples mated, including Maddie and Marcon. There is nothing like facing death to make you realize your feelings for someone else.

"Sarah, look at that lake! Have you ever seen anything like it?" I asked the woman I knew was my future mate.

"That's beautiful! How is the water purple? Is it contaminated?" Sarah asked with furrowed brow.

"No, there is an algae native to this planet that causes the lake waters to be purple. It is safe for you to swim in. Just do not drink the water." I took her hand and walked her to the shore.

She took off her shoes and walked in. "Come in, the water is really warm." She waved me over to join her. "I'm so glad you invited me here today! This is going to be a wonderful day!"

I walked up behind her and wrapped my arm around her tiny waist. After I rested my chin on her head for a few minutes I whispered, "Any time spent with you is a wonderful day." She smiled and I could not resist leaning over further to kiss her neck.

While I was kissing her someone screamed out so loud, the nearby birds all fled from the surrounding bushes and trees.

"What was that?" Sarah turned in my arms and looked at me with wide eyes.

I turned around to see what was going on and noticed several guards made their way to the meadow where Marcon and his mate, Maddie, were huddled. I took Sarah's hand and walked her out of the water, hoping that she would be safe.

The guard closest to us had to have known what was going on. "What happened?"

"One Moment." He put his hand to his ear. Then I heard him speaking through his implant. I hated hearing one-sided conversations. You never knew what was really going on when you could only hear the person next to you and not the one on the comm.

"Captain, Marcon and Maddie found the remains of a few human bodies. It is obvious they were taken by the Zateelians. We have called for a shuttle to come and get all of the females and take them back to the settlement. You might want to ensure your mate's safety by putting her on the first one. There are too many here to make one trip," Nextar said.

"Yes, thank you. She will be in the first group." I walked back to where Sarah stood waiting for me. She kept trying to peak over the shoulders of the warriors in front of her.

"Sarah, we have to go back to the settlement, it is not safe here. Marcon just discovered the remains of humans who had been attacked by the Zateelians. The shuttle is coming to pick you and some others up. I need you to be on the first shuttle." I wrapped my arms around her and drew her near. The intent was to comfort her, but in the end, it comforted me as well.

The idea of leaving her here all alone worried me. If I took another assignment and Sarah stayed her, what would happen to her? Our warriors would protect her like they protect the rest of the settlement. However, I could protect her better than anyone. She would be safe with me and loved like no one else could.

Sarah was my mate, if only she would realize I was hers.

Staying with Venay was the better move. I had made the correct decision to turn down my own ship, today only proved that she needed me to look after her. This planet is still too dangerous for humans. It's even too dangerous for warriors to be out on their own until we exterminate the Zateelians.

When the shuttle arrived I took Sarah straight to it. She was one of the first to hop aboard. "Eereen, what are you doing," she asked when I turned to join the warriors in the field.

"I have to stay and fight." I gave her a half smile and took in her beautiful features. Sarah had long blonde hair, blue eyes, and a healthy complexion. She spent time in the sun here, and it showed. However, she also used care to ensure she did not burn. However, there were a few sun kisses speckled across her nose, which just added to her charm. I was determined to make it back to her so I could kiss each and every one of them.

She jumped out and ran to me. "Don't leave me." Public displays of affection were frowned upon for warriors, especially senior officers. At that moment, I didn't care.

Sarah jumped into my arms and kissed me deeply and passionately in front of everyone. What could I do? I had to return her kiss. I felt the passion coming from her through our tenuous bond. My veins had to be pulsing red. I wanted nothing more than to take her and make her my mate right then and there. I had to stop this madness before I did something I would regret so I pulled back panting.

My mate was breathing heavily too. "Eereen, you better come back to me, alive and well. I'll never forgive you for leaving me alone on this alien world if you don't." She gave me one last hug and jumped on the shuttle. She took a seat next to the open door. I watched her as everyone else got on board. My feet refused to move until she was in the air and safely away.

"Nice, Captain." Nextar patted my shoulder and laughed. I followed him to the clearing where we heard the chittering of the bugs. Stars! Why do I use so many Earth terms now! I heard the Zateelians getting closer and my warriors went into action.

www.ingramcontent.com/pod-product-compliance
Lightning Source LLC
Chambersburg PA
CBHW030624190726